SHELEG

SHELEG

RONEN STAMBOULI

iUniverse, Inc.
New York Bloomington

Sheleg

iUniverse books may be ordered through booksellers or by contacting:

iUniverse
1663 Liberty Drive
Bloomington, IN 47403
www.iuniverse.com
1-800-Authors (1-800-288-4677)

ISBN: 978-0-595-52446-4 (sc)
ISBN: 978-0-595-62500-0 (ebook)

Printed in the United States of America

iUniverse rev. date: 03/27/2009

333

To my parents, Alberto and Esther, for more than giving me life—for allowing me to be who I am.

To my sister, Elia, and my brother, Ori, for letting me be the one in the middle.

To Alan, Eric, and Natasha, for giving me with the opportunity of being a father.

To Nunziata, my soul mate, for reminding me every day the true meaning of unconditional love, patience, and caring.

The stubborn don't learn;
the stubborn suffer.

Patience is a virtue of those who know what they are doing.
(Apathy is a false interpretation of this saying.)

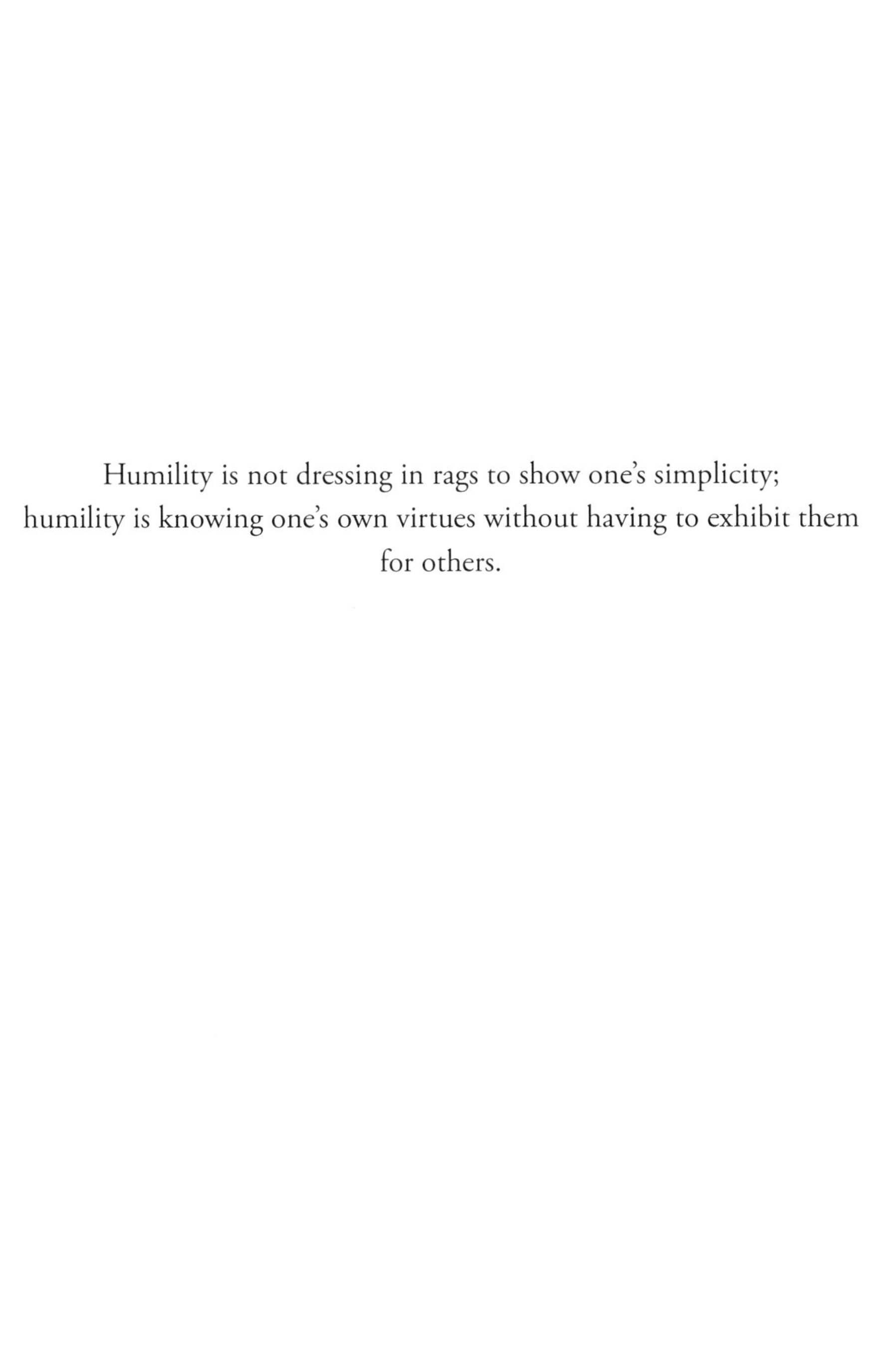

Humility is not dressing in rags to show one's simplicity;
humility is knowing one's own virtues without having to exhibit them
for others.

We were not made from money and riches;
we were created from thought and energy.

Contents

Preface

I was sitting in my living room one morning, and it was very quiet. My wife and children were still asleep. I started thinking about some of the things that had happened in my life, and I focused on one event in particular. I asked myself, *What would have happened if…*? I let myself go, and suddenly the chapters of this book flooded into my mind, one after the other. In less than twenty minutes, I had it all in my head.

It was fascinating to see how it all sprang up out of "nothing." I put that word in quotes because just where we think there isn't anything is where there is actually the most. And I emphasize this because even though we often say that seeing is believing, probably the reverse is the real truth: you have to believe to see.

I got up and went to the den, sat down in front of the computer, and began to write. After two hours, I had something I had always wanted: a story to tell—but even more important than that, a message to give.

There was just one little problem: I'm not a writer, and I've never published a book. *What do I do*? I wondered, since even though I had the characters, story line, and content all in my head (in the literal sense), in terms of what I had actually written, the book was a disaster.

I knew that actually doing the writing would be the greatest challenge. So I decided to just have faith in myself and in whatever had sent this story to me, since I knew it would show me the way, step by step, guiding me until I had finished what had once seemed impossible.

And that's just how it was. After a year of work, that little voice inside that helps guide you into the unknown had helped me to finish this book, magically presenting all the people that would help and support me along the way at just the right times.

What will happen now? That's an unknown that will only be made clear over time. That's how life is: little by little, things are revealed, and little by little, we learn. I hope this will be an opportunity for me to become closer to you and everyone who wishes for a better world to live in, and also the start of a new journey, with new challenges, new lessons, and especially, many good friends.

Introduction

When Sheleg was twenty-one, tragedy changed the course of his life. The explosion of two bombs in Kuta, a tourist town on the island of Bali, damaged some buildings and destroyed some others completely. Beneath the ruins lay the bodies of the revelers who had been peacefully enjoying the night.

Minutes before the explosions, Sheleg stopped on a corner just a few blocks away from the small café where his friends Mia, Charley, and Ely were waiting for him.

Then the first explosion rocked the area. Sheleg saw a cloud of smoke and dust rising from the buildings near the café where his friends were. He quickly crossed the street and headed for the café, but a second explosion, even bigger than the first, stopped him in his tracks before he could get very far.

When he got to the site of the explosions, he couldn't believe his eyes; the scene of horror and panic was just as dramatic as the destruction. Entire buildings had been reduced to ruins. Cars that had caught fire gave rise to thick, black plumes of smoke, and dozens of wounded—surrounded by the dead—wandered in a daze, shocked and disoriented, trying to make sense of what had just happened.

Sheleg fell to his knees, while all around him people ran hysterically from one place to another. Something told him there was nothing to be done; he knew his friends were not there anymore. He sat down in the middle of the street and stayed there for hours, unable to move, completely disconnected.

Several months later, Sheleg went back there. The area had been partially rebuilt, and even though it still bore the signs of what had happened, life went on. The tourists had returned, injecting new life into that decimated place.

The sun was setting as Sheleg walked into the renovated café where his three friends had gathered for the last time. He approached the owner, an older, kind-looking man, and with tears in his eyes he promised him that he would spend the rest of his life searching for peace and delivering its message. The man stepped toward Sheleg and embraced him tightly. Whispering a blessing, he forever sealed Sheleg's vow.

Sheleg never could have imagined what destiny had in store for him …

CHAPTER 1

Reconnecting

"Don't be afraid to be different from everyone else.
Be afraid to be different from yourself."

Everyone creates their own reality,
often without even realizing it.

~ ~ ~

Twenty years later…

Sheleg was getting out of a taxi on a busy Manhattan street, saying goodbye to Hassan, the cab driver. Hassan had decided not to charge Sheleg for the ride, since their conversation had been worth much more than the few dollars showing on the taxi's meter. And even though it sounds like something out of a fantasy novel—a cab driver in New York City not charging a thing for his services—this was a special case.

"It was a pleasure meeting you. Thank you, and God bless you!" the friendly Arabic man said with a smile.

"The feeling is mutual, and don't forget that your fears cannot stand in the way of your family's future, because each one of them is a free spirit. They need to learn and have their own experiences. Remember … love sets free; it doesn't oppress."

"I'll remember that." Hassan said, nodding, and waved good-bye.

Sheleg stepped back, and they smiled at each other as the cab pulled away from the curb.

It was a lovely spring morning. Sheleg gazed up at the skyscrapers that rose impressively all around him. He felt free, fresh, and full of energy; the city was having quite an effect on him. He had never been there before. Even though the constant thrum of activity that seemed to emanate even from the walls of the buildings never stopped for a minute, he was enjoying New York's frenetic pace. He watched people rushing by, walking in all directions, and saw steam from the subway rising up from grates in the streets. He saw several food vendors on the sidewalks and smelled the mix of aromas from each one. He saw businessmen in suits and ties, Orthodox Jews in their black hats and coats, even a homeless man directing traffic in the middle of the street as he warned anyone within earshot that the end of the world was fast approaching.

Sheleg happily soaked it all in as he looked toward the end of the avenue and wondered, *What is it that's calling me to this city? What is pushing me to visit Jose here after all these years*? The unfathomable answer would only be revealed later, further on down the road.

He had been traveling the world for several years now. After what had happened in Indonesia, he had decided to set off in search of his life's purpose. He sensed that in the wake of that horrible tragedy, there must be some way to find peace and happiness.

With the passing of the years, Sheleg found that he had not been mistaken. He learned that peace and happiness were not some prize handed out randomly to the lucky few; they were more like states of mind that could be found in the spirit and essence of every human being—if they sought them. Sheleg found the answers to his questions in the countless trips he had made all over the world; every city and every town, every mountain, every forest represented a new life experience, a new lesson, a new answer.

That restless search and everything he had experienced along the way: life and death, hatred and anger, hunger and thirst, sex and drugs, as well as peace and love, kisses and caresses, truth and wisdom—all allowed him to finally understand the true nature of things and the real origins of everything. He learned that the three fundamentals of human existence are love, a positive attitude toward life, and sharing. These three qualities, Sheleg discovered, provided the necessary peace and clarity to see what path to take, guided by one's inner voice and one's instincts.

He remembered the words of a cheerful shaman: "We came into this world to be happy and to grow, knowing that we are solely responsible for what happens in our lives. Nothing is circumstantial; everything arises from our own thoughts and feelings, and when we finally find our reason for being, our lives can transform into a rich abundance of achievements and blessings."

Over time, Sheleg also sharpened his ability of perception, giving him a clear perspective on the existential reality of people's lives. People, when in doubt, would flock to him for advice and support. His wish to give the best of himself drove him to move from place to place. This time his destination was Manhattan, to reconnect with a wonderful childhood friend, Jose Lombardi.

In the weeks before his arrival in New York, Sheleg had been thinking about Jose quite a bit. His inner voice repeatedly called up his old friend's name, and something told him that he should try and get in touch with Jose. Through several friends in common, Sheleg was able to contact him—since time and distance had pulled them in different directions—and they stayed in touch until an opportunity came up for Sheleg to travel to New York.

A gentle breeze circulated around the skyscrapers, softly brushing everything in its path while Sheleg, carrying a small shoulder bag and wearing jeans and a tee shirt, stepped through a giant revolving door. This building housed the offices of J. L. Investments, his friend Jose's real estate company. He walked through the cavernous lobby, with its handsome, marble floors and elegant, multicolored glass windows, and greeted the young man behind the reception desk with a smile. "Hello, I'm here to see Mr. Lombardi."

"Very well, sir," the dark-skinned man said cheerfully. "Just sign in here, and take the elevator on your right. Go up to the thirty-third floor; his group's offices are there."

As Sheleg signed the visitor's log, he noticed a magazine on jazz music behind the counter. There was a CD player next to it, and he became aware of the jazz piece playing on it.

"You like jazz, right?" he asked the guard as he finished filling in the log.

"Ohhh, yes," he replied, eager to continue the conversation. "Nothing can compare to the melodies in jazz. Listen to this; I wrote this piece myself." He turned up the volume, swaying to the music. "This is my band. We play every two weeks at the Big Jazz Bar."

"It sounds great!" Sheleg nodded along to the beat. "I've heard of that place, the Big Jazz. I play guitar. I like Gambale, Beck … maybe someday we can play together!" he said, smiling, inspired by the friendly guard.

"No problem. As soon as I'm done with this awful job, we can get together."

"I understand," Sheleg said, seeing the look of frustration on the man's face.

"I do want to get out of this so I can just play music full time and not have to sit here day and night while life passes me by. Oh, the missed opportunities … but I have to make a living."

"Of course," Sheleg replied, picking up on his emotions as he kept talking.

"But someday, brother, someday it's gonna happen, and everything's gonna be different. It's only a matter of time and you'll see the ads in all the papers: 'Terry La-Clede and his Jazz Band, Live!'"

"I hope it really does happen, because this record is really good," Sheleg said. "Have you been working here long?"

"Next week it will have been two years and seven months since I started." He sighed heavily, crossing his arms and leaning back in his chair.

The exactness of Terry's answer and his body language helped complete the image of the guard's life that had begun to take shape in Sheleg's mind. He had spent almost three years working as a guard, day and night. He couldn't spend the time he wanted to on his music, his band, and more than anything, his dreams.

"Why don't you make that day—the day it's gonna happen—today, right now?"

"How?" the guard asked, his eyes wide, leaning back even farther in his chair.

"You just said your life and your dreams are slipping away as you sit there in that chair. If you don't like sitting there, it means that maybe you shouldn't be sitting there. Listen to what your heart wants, and do what it tells you. That's the only way to get to where you really want to go. Until you do, you'll keep on being a prisoner of this job, because you think it's the only way to make a living."

"Yeah, but that's not easy," Terry said, resigned. "Look, my wife says I'm a dreamer too, and that we're not going to get anywhere just dreaming. I feel like I'm trapped between a rock and a hard place. She's been such a big support to me, and I don't want to disappoint her. That's why I don't take a step forward. I don't want to lose the little we have now and make things worse. But on the other hand, I think she's right, and I should do something to change my life even though I'm afraid of failing and having to come back to this job in the end … that would be so frustrating. Do you understand?"

"Of course," said Sheleg. "And that's the point—you haven't been able to convince yourself of your own potential because of your fear of failure. So it's understandable that your wife would feel that way. You need to get your priorities in order. Convert your dreams into action and stop just thinking about them."

"Right, but how?"

"Have faith in yourself and in what you want. If life gave you a talent, then live through it, because that is what you're meant to do. And don't worry about the future so much, because that can be a distraction and fill us with doubts. Visualize your goals. Start by taking small steps, and you'll see how the path you should take will become clear to you, and doors will start to open."

Terry looked at him thoughtfully and nodded in agreement, stroking his chin. After a moment he said, "Yes. I can't deny it. I'm afraid to take that first step, since my whole life I've been scared of failing." He paused before saying, "I don't know why I'm telling all this to a stranger, but it's probably because when I was growing up, I saw how my dad was so unappreciated by my mother. She was always saying what a failure he was. I'll never forget lying in my bed when I was little, listening to her humiliate him all the time. He was a good man, and he always did everything he could for us, but she never knew how to appreciate it …" His voice was sad, and his heavy expression did nothing to conceal his unhappiness.

Sheleg sighed. Smiling encouragingly, he said deliberately, "Our parents are a part of our story, but they're not the whole story, because we all have our own part to tell. So don't take criticisms that were not meant for you to heart. You should just learn from those experiences so you can change what caused you so much pain, and not repeat it."

There was a short pause until Terry spoke again. "Yes, it's true. I know what you mean. But the fears are still there. They follow you; they become a part of you."

"Fears are understandable, and even necessary, because they let us move forward cautiously. So we have to just accept them as part of the process, but not as an insurmountable obstacle. Otherwise they will control us, and we'll stay stuck in the same place, unable to make any progress."

There was a gleam in Terry's eye as the guard reached out to shake the hand of the man who had certainly helped to show him the way. "Yes, you're right. Thanks so much for talking with me. It was really great to hear some encouragement, especially from somebody who doesn't know me and can be objective."

"For me, meeting you has been a privilege," Sheleg said. "And one more thing—if you don't mind, can you sign this? I'd like to have it as a souvenir." Sheleg reached into his bag and took out a CD sleeve.

"Of course, my brother! This autograph is really going to be worth something in a few years, you'll see!" he said as he picked up a pen and tried to sign it, but with no luck. "I think this pen's out of ink," he said as he shook it and made some scribbles on a plain white envelope. "Okay, now it works!" Terry said brightly as the ink started flowing and he wrote his name on the envelope. He then finally autographed Sheleg's CD sleeve and handed it back to him. "Take good care of it; you never know …"

"I will! Thank you," Sheleg said as he smiled, happy to have had the chance to meet this fascinating man.

"Let's keep in touch. It was great meeting you, and good luck with everything."

"You too … now, what floor am I going to again?" he asked, putting the CD back in his bag.

"The thirty-third floor. The elevator's there on your right."

Sheleg smiled. That number was a sure sign that everything was under control. The numbers three, thirty-three, and three-hundred and thirty-three had been assigned to him by fate to tell him he was on the right path. Every time they spontaneously appeared in his life, he knew everything was as it should be. Coincidences were just a part of the universal lexicon that told him which direction to take.

"Very interesting," he said to himself as he pressed the button in the elevator. "Now let's see what's in store."

In a few seconds the elevator doors opened onto a well-appointed reception area. Behind the desk sat a beautiful woman with black hair and big, hazel eyes who was wearing a headset. "Good morning. I'm here to see Jose Lombardi. My name is Sheleg," he said, appreciating the young woman's beauty.

"Oh, yes! Please, follow me, he's waiting for you," she said with a smile as she got up from behind the desk and led the way.

"Thank you," he said, following her down a long hallway and trying not to openly stare at the attractive young woman. He felt a light current of cool air as they walked and heard the muted voices and footsteps of the people who worked on that floor. There were two long, parallel hallways running the length of the floor, which were interconnected by shorter hallways. The many small offices all had glass windows, so everyone could be easily seen as they worked.

"Jennifer! Please tell Mr. Lombardi that the McKaslin report is ready!" said a woman in her sixties. It was Joanne, the chief administrative officer of the company. She had been Jose's right hand ever since he had started up his real estate business in a tiny office on the outskirts of Brooklyn.

"Okay," the receptionist said, pausing in the doorway to Joanne's office to make sure she had heard her.

"Thanks! And when you have a minute, please give me the number of your friend again—the hairdresser. I think I lost it."

Jennifer nodded while the cheerful older woman asked, "Can I assume this handsome man is Jose's friend?"

"Yes," Jennifer said, smiling.

"Very nice to meet you," Sheleg interjected. "You must be Joanne, right? Jose has told me so much about you."

"Yes, that's me," she said. "But don't believe a word he's said about me! Especially if he mentioned that I'm married," she said with a devilish smile as she folded some papers on her desk and reached over to answer her ringing telephone.

Jennifer and Sheleg laughed and continued on down the hall.

"That Joanne sure is a character," Jennifer said, grinning.

"Yes, I noticed. Jose told me that he couldn't survive without her, that she keeps the whole office organized."

"That's true; everything in this office has her fingerprints all over it! You have no idea."

"How long have you been working here?" he asked. His thoughts briefly turned to his wife, Michelle. Like him, the word "jealous" was not in her vocabulary since their love was real and they both knew how to respect their relationship.

"I started here just a little while ago. I graduated from college a few months ago, and they needed somebody here to help Joanne out, so I jumped at the opportunity. It sounded like an interesting place to work. And what about you? Will you be in New York long?" she asked as she turned left and led him toward Jose's office.

"I'll definitely be here for a few days. We'll see exactly how long depending on how things go …" he answered, trailing off as they walked into a very spacious, smartly designed office.

"Mr. Lombardi, it's Mr.—" Jennifer didn't finish as Jose interrupted her, waving with his hand. He was in the middle of a heated telephone conversation. He puffed on a cigarette, apparently trying to control his rising stress. At the same time, he gripped the remote control to the nearby television, clicking through channels randomly. Just then, a cell phone on his desk started to ring. Jennifer went over to answer it, but as she reached for it she brushed a huge stack of papers, knocking it over and burying the phone, and the call was lost. Sheleg observed the chaotic scene and had to smile at the sight. This was all very atypical for him, since he didn't even own a cellular phone, and he certainly didn't have an office. The few worldly possessions he had were all in the bag he carried with him.

Jose no longer had the youthful face that Sheleg remembered from their teenage years, although he still had the same sardonic air. It was strange to see him, after so many years, wearing a tie, looking so serious, and with graying hair. This new image contrasted completely with his younger self from all those years ago: the disheveled, shoulder-length hair, his leather jacket with the peace sign on it, and the marijuana joint the two used to smoke together in the city park or on the university campus.

Sheleg sat down on a leather sofa in front of the window and looked down at the panorama of New York City spread out before him. He quietly admired the view as his friend kept talking on the phone.

The scene he contemplated through the window was very impressive. The skyscrapers, the Statue of Liberty in the distance, the bridges … he enjoyed simply taking in the iconic view, which he had only ever seen before in movies and on postcards. He had heard so much about the city, and for the first time in his life he could see it for himself. He was very impressed by the architecture, and he thought it was wonderful to be able to witness yet again how far human imagination and ambition could go. Thousands of buildings, each with its own personality and style, rose up from one end of the city to the other.

As his gaze drifted off to the horizon, it occurred to Sheleg that these manmade creations were often not in harmony with nature. Much of what man had been able to achieve came at the cost of a crucial balance that the species hadn't yet learned how to measure. Sheleg thought that since we had not learned how to effectively manage our responsibility, we were threatening the stability of the entire planet.

Jose finished up his phone conversation as he stared down at his desk, irritated and shaking his head. His agitation was understandable. Apparently the new management deal for a commercial complex in which he had invested considerable time and money was already on the point of collapsing, all because of a ridiculous bureaucratic technicality. But this was all in a day's work for Jose, who had founded one of the most prestigious real estate companies in New York City. He was a much-admired entrepreneur and he couldn't complain about his life, although he knew that all of his achievements came at a very high price: long work hours, high stress levels, vacations that were always interrupted, and even health problems like high blood pressure and sporadic panic attacks.

There was Jose, stressed out, still ruminating over the conversation he had just finished, as Sheleg wondered, *Alright, let's see how long it takes for Jose to look at me and say, "Hey, Sheleg, great to see you."*

And just then Jose looked up and, pushing his frustration aside, said happily, "Hey, Sheleg, how are you?" He got up and gave Sheleg a big hug. "How many years has it been?" Jose said, gripping Sheleg's shoulders. "It's so great to see you! I can't believe it! Here, sit down. Can I get you something to drink?"

"Just water, thank you."

"And a coffee for me." Jose looked at Jennifer as she finished gathering up some papers that had slipped off of his desk.

"No problem. I'll be right back," she said politely as she left the office.

"Now tell me, are you going to stay with us here, or do you have other plans?" Jose asked.

"Aside from just seeing you, I don't have any plans. I thought it was important to see you, so here I am."

"I'm glad you're here. We have so much to talk about after all these years," Jose said. He considered Sheleg's answer and then asked, "I hope you don't mind my asking, but since the last time we talked I've been wondering, is something going on with you?"

"Something like what?" Sheleg asked, turning to face the window.

"I don't know. Some kind of problem? Maybe you're under some kind of deadline, since you said you thought it was important to see me now, but you haven't said why," Jose replied as he stood beside his friend, looking out through the thick glass across the city.

"No, actually, everything's going great; there's nothing going on. And to make sure things continue to be great, I think it's important that we're right here where we are at this very moment," he said somewhat cryptically. He didn't think it was the right moment to get into too much detail.

"Oh, really?" Jose asked, puzzled. "Now I'm even more confused. Why did you come here, anyway?"

"That's the thing; I don't know exactly. I'm … searching for something." Sheleg smiled, knowing he wasn't exactly clearing things up. "But right now, even I don't know what that something could be.

We'll just see what happens … but let's talk about that some other time. After so many years I'd rather talk about other things right now."

"Could it be something bad?" Jose persisted, unwilling to drop the subject.

"Hey, what's with all the questions? Don't worry about it; it's nothing bad. It never is, thank God. Well, in general it isn't," he said enigmatically, making light of his friend's confusion.

"Alright, alright," Jose said, raising his hands. He began to remember his old friend's sense of humor. "We'll leave it like that for the moment. If I didn't know you better I'd think you were losing your mind. Come with me, I want to show you around the company. You'll see what a loony bin this place is. People are always interrupting me, I never get five minutes to myself, and if I don't give them an answer right away you wouldn't believe what a mess it is."

Jose straightened up a few things on his desk before they left. His thoughts lost in the past, he said, "When I saw you come through the door, the first thing I thought of was how we used to get high in the university courtyard, and those backpacking trips we used to take. That was quite a time, wasn't it?"

"Yes, of course. I was thinking about those times, too," Sheleg said, putting an arm around his friend as they walked down the hall. "And you just reminded me of a trip I took to the Amazon three years ago with Michelle. We spent several days with a tribe called the Xinguanos, and at one of their nighttime ritual festivals, they gave us a small, steaming bowl with a very strange odor rising from it. We breathed it in, like the rest of the tribe, and within a few minutes we were laughing uncontrollably. All the people started dancing and singing and carrying on, telling stories. The party went on all night."

"That sounds really interesting! Sounds like they have a good life. Was it one of those tribes that walk around naked and paint their bodies?" Jose asked, laughing.

"Yes, all the tribes in that area are like that," Sheleg explained as several people walked by them in the hall.

"And how did you understand them?"

"We had a young man with us to translate; he was a native from a town called Leticia, near the Amazon River. He was something like an adopted son of the tribe, and he explained everything to us as it happened. He was the one who guided us to that place."

"That's fascinating. Of everything you saw there, what made the biggest impression?" Jose asked.

"How they raise their children," Sheleg replied after a pause. "They were always happy, playing and running around. By the time they are twelve years old, they are considered adults and they have learned all the knowledge and traditions of their tribe."

"Fascinating ..." Jose repeated as he patted his pockets, vainly searching for the pack of cigarettes he had left behind on his desk.

"Yes, it really was fascinating. Punishment doesn't exist there, for children or adults. I remember a story that Balao, our translator told us. He said that once when a boy had set a hut on fire, they'd formed a human chain to carry water from the river. Everyone was shouting and even laughing. Even though the damage was very serious, the boy was not punished at all. They explained that the boy could have done it just because he was a child—it was part of his world. They even started calling him "Conomét Aratá" as a joke, which in their language means "Fire Boy."

"You've got to be kidding! If one of my kids did that I'd kill him!" Jose chuckled.

"Well, it just goes to show what things are like in cultures that are supposedly more 'primitive' than ours."

"Does that Balao guy live there among those people?" Jose queried.

"Yes, he decided his world was with them, and he left the village of Leticia. Little by little, he integrated into the tribe. We had been staying with his family, and they had told us about how Balao had gone off to live in the Amazon. He happened to come back to visit his family while we were staying with them. Michelle and I got along really well with him, and then he took the two of us back with him to meet the tribe—"

"See, that," Jose interrupted, "that's just the kind of thing that I really miss. That freedom, the adventures, seeing the world like that. Sometimes I wonder if all of this is really worth it. I don't mean I'm not happy, but sometimes you can get stuck in your own ambition, and when you try to go back to how things were before, it's like all the doors you went through to get to where you are slammed shut after you got to the other side, and there's no way back."

Sheleg listened, understanding his friend's reality. "Nothing is irreversible, Jose. It's just a matter of finding a balance and putting your priorities in order."

As they ambled down the hallway, phones rang, photocopiers worked at full speed, and the ubiquitous mugs of coffee on every desk seemed to Sheleg to be the common denominator in that office.

"Yes, you're right," Jose said. "I always thought that once I had money, I'd be free. But the reality is I've created a big, complex structure, and it seems to trap me a little more every day."

"Get your priorities in order," Sheleg said again. "You should visualize what you really need, and not so much what you want. It's very important to understand the difference, because we often tend to confuse the two, and that's when we run into trouble."

"Yes, you might be right about that. We want so many things in life, and then once we finally get them, we realize that it's not what we need. I think I know exactly what you mean."

They toured Jose's floor of the office, chatting the whole time. After a while they came to face a bank of elevators. "Can we take the stairs?" Sheleg asked.

"Sure we could," Jose replied, perplexed. "But the elevator's more comfortable," he quickly added.

"Then we should take the stairs."

Not knowing what his friend's motives were, Jose shrugged and headed for the stairwell. "I don't really get around to this side of the building much, but you know something? It was a good idea. The atmosphere's a bit different—I'll have to remember that."

Then Jose almost collided with a young man in the hallway. He was a tall man with a friendly expression. He looked Caribbean, with a light brown complexion, deep, green eyes, and curly hair that fell to his shoulders.

"Oh, sorry, Mr. Lombardi," he said.

"It's nothing, I'm used to it."

Sheleg looked intently at the young man and asked, "Have you ever been in Kamptagua?"

Smiling broadly, he said, "Yeah, I was there last year for the Waipoua Kauri Festival."

"That's what I thought." Sheleg held out his hand. "I'm Sheleg, and I'm here visiting New York."

"I'm Gabriel," the young man replied, and he looked at Jose, who looked confused. Gabriel explained, "This amulet I'm wearing is something they give you on Kamptagua Island. It's a tradition; everyone who goes there gets one."

"Okay, now I get it. Where is that place?" Jose asked.

"It's very far away, where the Tasman Sea meets the Pacific Ocean, north of Australia and New Zealand. The only way to get there is by water, and not too many people know the way … it's kind of complicated. But if it's your destiny to go there, you'll definitely make it," Gabriel concluded.

"And what is that festival you mentioned all about?"

"It's a celebration they have on the island once a year to give thanks to the forests. Waipoua Kauri is a forest, and they use the name symbolically."

"So why is it so complicated to get there?" Jose asked, the picture becoming clearer.

"It's not that it's complicated, exactly; it's just that not everybody is supposed to go there. According to tradition, only people with a level of energy that they call 'gamma' can be invited to the island. They're afraid of 'modern' man's influence, because he always imposes his own lifestyle, which is in many ways directly opposed to theirs."

"Are the people there Indians with painted bodies and bows and arrows, too?" Jose asked, remembering Sheleg's story about the Amazonian tribe.

"No, not at all," Gabriel answered. "Even though it's a small island without many technological advances, they have learned how to blend aspects of their traditional lifestyle with certain aspects of modern life. For example, they use energy from nature to produce electricity without having any negative effects on their environment, using windmills and water wheels in the river. But on the other hand, they don't use telephones, televisions, or computers anywhere on the island. There are only two vehicles on the entire island for everyone, which people can use only when it's absolutely necessary."

"How do they live? What are their houses like?" Jose asked, curious.

"Their houses look like a cross between a pagoda and a chalet, they look kind of Javanese. They're really nice looking and very cozy, decorated with wood from fallen trees and painted with paint they make themselves from flowers they grow," Gabriel explained.

"Actually they have everything they need in their houses: bedrooms, bathrooms, fireplaces for the winter—and they have big, open common areas, with rugs and tapestries," Sheleg expounded. "All around there are lots of palm trees that have been crossed with golden zarzo wildflowers, which are typical of the region of Australia, and which give the countryside there a very striking appearance."

"And they are gifted rock sculptors," Gabriel added. "You can see it all around the island. There's one lighthouse that's fifty feet tall, and they made it with three giant rocks. It's just amazing. The hills on the island are covered with a kind of grass that you find all over the island, reaching even the edges of the beaches."

Jose said, "I would imagine they raise their own food, right?"

"Yes, they spend a lot of time on raising crops. They say it's the best way to stay healthy," Gabriel explained.

"So how did you get to the island?" Jose asked.

"I was trying to find some tourist information on a place called Cabo Reinga, in the north of New Zealand. I was talking to someone for a long time; he was very helpful. He told me about the island, which was where he lived, and offered to take me there. We went in his boat, traveling for almost six hours until we finally got there in the middle of the night."

"And how about you, Sheleg? How did you get there?" Jose asked his friend.

"It was a similar situation. I was in the north of New Zealand too, in an area called Hararu. I was talking to a group of people who were performing rituals in the river. They described their life on the island, and they took me there to see it."

"But weren't you scared?" Jose asked.

"Not at all! These people are so deeply spiritual, they radiate it, and you don't doubt them for a second. They have a history of over one thousand, five hundred years on the island," Gabriel said.

"One thousand, five hundred years?" Jose exclaimed. "That's a long time! What do you mean they're deeply spiritual?"

"To give an example, they live in harmony on the island with wild animals; they don't bother each other. For centuries, the people of the island have based their relationship with the animals on not exploiting them or using them to benefit themselves," Gabriel explained.

"Wow! I wonder if the kids there have pet tigers!" Jose said, and they all laughed. "Maybe someday I can go there, too."

"Of course!" Gabriel said, but he started to turn away. "I'd better get going, though. They're waiting for these documents in the office," he explained.

"It was so nice meeting you. I'm sure we'll see each other again and we can talk more," Sheleg said.

"Of course. When the moon is full, lighting up the sky, we'll meet again," he said, giving Sheleg the thumbs-up as he walked away.

"What a coincidence, right?" Jose said, raising his eyebrows.

"Yes, I was just thinking about that. I see this meeting as a sign that our presence here is no accident. Coincidences are like a kind of language that the universe uses to communicate with us and tell us things. You just have to pay attention and understand how they relate to what is going on."

"So you think this coincidence has to do with what brought you to New York?" Jose asked.

"Yes, I'm sure of it."

"That's why you didn't want to take the elevator? You knew you would meet somebody here!"

"Well … I didn't exactly know I was going to meet somebody here. It's just that something told me to take the stairs, and I obeyed that voice. I didn't question or analyze it, I just obeyed it."

"Okay … and if that voice told you to jump out a window on the thirty-third floor? Would you do that, too?" Jose asked, skeptical.

Sheleg replied, "When your main objective, in your heart and mind, is the common good, free of all negativity, you can be sure that those kinds of thoughts will not even enter your head. Faith is not reflexively challenging the laws of the universe, but rather it's understanding them and knowing how to put them to good use."

Jose smiled at his friend, put an arm around his shoulder, and said, "Yeah, you're right. It's so good to see you again! Let's go back to my office; I want to call Mary and see if we can all have dinner tonight. What do you think?" Jose asked.

"That sounds perfect. I'll spend the rest of the day walking around the city, and you can get back to work."

More than an hour had passed since Sheleg had first arrived in the building, and he felt it was time to go. He felt that from that moment on his presence was completely unnecessary, and so it was time to leave.

That was the balance of presence—knowing when to come and when to go so as not to threaten the harmony of any relationship.

He hugged Jose. Before he left, he teased, "I really like this place, it's so peaceful. I think I'll come to work with you one of these days."

Pensive, Jose realized that for over an hour he had completely disconnected from the constant hustle and bustle of his office. He remembered his own words about how hectic the office was and how he never went uninterrupted for five minutes. He was amazed that so much time had passed, yet no one had so much as stopped him to ask a quick question. Something was clearly going on here, and Jose was starting to understand, but he still rationalized it as just a coincidence. Just then his cell phone rang, and he quickly answered it.

"Hi, honey, just give me a minute—" he said in a rush, still puzzling over the lack of busyness. He shouted out to Sheleg, who was already walking down the hall, "Hey, Sheleg! It's Mary. I'm going to tell her that the three of us are having dinner at our place tonight!"

"Perfect," Sheleg said without even turning around, waving his hand in agreement as several employees brushed past him looking for Jose and as the businessman's cell phone rang again with a new call. Suddenly Jose was right back in the frenzied pace he had gotten so used to.

How did my Mary know I wanted to talk to her? he wondered as he put her on hold while he answered the other call and gestured to his employees to follow him into his office.

IIIIIIIIIII

A few minutes later, Sheleg left the building. He said good-bye to Terry behind the reception desk first and asked him if he could recommend a nearby café.

As Sheleg walked along the busy sidewalks, memories from his past came to mind. He especially thought of his three friends Mia, Charley, and Ely who had perished in the explosion in Bali—seeing Jose again had brought those memories to the surface since he had been a part of that circle of friends.

He came to the café Terry had mentioned and sat down at one of the tables outside. He ordered a cappuccino, and the irritated-looking waiter brought it to him a few minutes later. Sheleg reached into his bag and took out a copy of a letter he had written to a friend several years ago, after the events in Indonesia, in which he explained why the friends he had lost in the explosion meant so much to him.

IIIIIIIIIII

Dear Marcia:

I thought it was important to tell you this story, and make you a part of it. After you read it, you'll understand who these friends were, who you've heard me talk about so much. I haven't told you before because the wounds were still too fresh …

I was in the army, fulfilling my obligatory military service requirement. One night while we were out on patrol, we were ambushed by a group who wanted to invade a town and kill or kidnap the residents. That's what things are like here, as crazy as it sounds … and it's even harder to write about.

It was a cold winter night. It all happened at around 4:30 in the morning. We had received reports warning of a possible attack, and all units were on high alert; it was only a matter of time before it happened. We were exhausted from such a long patrol, since the night patrol extended on into the morning. Since we were on high alert, we weren't allowed to return to the base, so we had to stay on guard for many more hours.

The commanding officer in our vehicle ordered that we pull over to the side of the road for a few minutes to get some rest. I closed my eyes, but once I finally managed to get to sleep, we received the notice that there had been a security breach. Our driver started the jeep and we quickly drove to the area indicated. The cold wind blew harder than ever, masking the fact that I was trembling from nerves more than anything else.

Our commanding officer shouted orders from the front seat telling us what we had to do if we got into a confrontation, but to me his words were just sounds mixed with the howling of the wind. My head was in another place; my life was passing before my eyes. My family, my girlfriend, my friends ... they were all in the movie running through my mind, telling my life's story. I had the strangest feeling that everything was about to end and there was nothing I could do about it. I felt resigned, but that quickly turned into a survival instinct. For the first time in my life I was struck by the awesome meaning of existence, of family, friends.

When you are going to lose everything, things take on a new meaning that is very hard to explain. In a fraction of an instant, I remembered chatting with Ely and Charley when we were on a backpacking trip. I remembered talking with Mia at the lake the time we slept in a bus station because we'd been robbed. Those, and a thousand other memories, flashed in my mind, and I understood that more than just being my friends, those three were an integral part of me. I understood they were something I didn't want to let go of—I couldn't, and yet then in that jeep I felt that was exactly what was about to happen.

*There are no gray areas here. Suicide attacks are just that—*suicide *attacks—they had come here to die. Their goal was to take as many people with them as they possibly could, with their machine guns and grenades. Mindful of this bleak inevitability, at that moment all I wanted to do was see those people who had come here to destroy me and unload all the bullets I had into their bodies. It was the closest feeling to sheer savagery that I've ever experienced, and fortunately I never had it again.*

A few minutes later, I was wounded in the most horrific way you can imagine. I spent six months in the hospital and underwent twelve surgeries before I was finally released ...

IIIIIIIIIII

Lost in thought, Sheleg stopped reading. He gazed up at the sky and felt that his three dear friends were very close to him. He knew they were okay, and someday he would be with them again.

Just then a homeless man quietly approached him. Standing on the sidewalk behind the flower boxes that marked the café's limits, the man asked for some help so he could get something to eat.

Sheleg nodded, folded up his letter, and put it back in his bag. There was still much more written, but he thought he would read the rest of it later.

CHAPTER 2

The beggar

"Ambitions are possibilities;
expectations, possible frustrations."

When love, peace, and harmony
exist in us, we can attain truth and wisdom.
Only then will perfect abundance come into our lives.
Those who seek abundance without respecting these facts
will probably accumulate many things which,
in the long run, will not be worth all the chaos
caused by the effort to get them.

~ ~ ~

"Why don't you sit down?" Sheleg offered the beggar, gesturing to the chair across from him. "I'm not from here, and who better than you to tell me about the city."

"That's very nice of you, but if you could just give me some change, I can buy something somewhere else and not bother anybody here."

"I understand," Sheleg said, just as the waiter came over and glared at the beggar.

"Please just get out of here," the ill-tempered waiter said. "Go on, go on. Go panhandle somewhere else; you're bothering the customers."

Sheleg turned to the waiter and asked, "Do you mind if the gentleman sits here with me if I buy him something?"

Looking even more irritated, the waiter replied, "Look, my friend, if you want to hand out charity and feed bums, go ahead; it's not my problem. But do it somewhere else. This isn't a soup kitchen. Alright?"

"Alright, no problem. How much do I owe you for the cappuccino?"

"It's three twenty-five," he sneered.

While Sheleg opened his bag to take out the money, the beggar handed a ten-dollar bill to the waiter over the flower box. The arrogant waiter just looked at it, completely taken aback. "Just take it; it won't bite you!" the beggar said to the stunned waiter. Unsure, he slowly took the bill as the old man continued, "For some reason, I must deserve everything that's happened to me, and people like you are just doing your job and reminding me of this. Don't feel guilty for what you do … just feel guilty for having been chosen to play this part."

The waiter, trying to evade the moment, rapidly said, "I'll be right back with your change."

"That's okay, young man. You should save that bill. It's worth much more than the cup of coffee you just served," the old man said as he turned to Sheleg. He finished, "Like everything in life, that ten-dollar bill has a story, too."

Grappling with his own selfishness, the waiter turned and went inside without another word, grasping the bill.

"Thanks," said Sheleg with a warm smile that helped them to get past the ugly incident as they left together. "See that? I ended up being the guest!"

"That's what you learn in the streets, boy—you never know how life is going to turn things around for you."

Sheleg looked closely at the old man. He listened carefully to every word, since he had learned that knowledge acquired in the street should be listened to. The beggar went on, "Bah! I don't care about being accepted at that place, and I understand that nobody wants to be near a smelly beggar. I've gotten used to the scorn and rejection. But still, humiliating another person will always seem grotesque to me, no matter who it is."

"What's that ten-dollar bill's story?" Sheleg asked.

"Sit down and I'll tell you."

They both sat down side by side on the sidewalk, leaning against a building, and the beggar began to tell his story.

"Once, I was sitting right here in this spot, and a woman walked by with her young son. He stared at me as they went by, and I heard him innocently ask his mother why I was so dirty and messy. I didn't hear her answer as they walked away and out of my sight. A few minutes later, the boy came running back to me, his mother watching him from down the block. 'Here, mister,' he said, and he gave me a dollar. 'Thank you, son, and God bless you,' I replied, very touched.

"He just looked at me for a minute, and then he said, 'No, mister, God should bless you, not me, because my mom told me you're poor, and you don't have a house, and maybe you don't have a mom, either.' I just looked back at him without a word, because I knew if I tried to speak, I couldn't hold in my tears. The little boy continued, 'Do you think that will be enough to buy a house and a mom?'

"'I think so, son,' I said, and smiled at the boy. Gazing back at me, he reached into his pocket. 'I've been saving this to buy a present for my mom. She doesn't know, but in case that's not enough, you can use this, too,' he said sweetly, and handed me a ten-dollar bill.

"Well I was so taken aback by this that it took a moment for me to say, 'Thank you; you're a very good boy. And when God comes to bless me, I'm going to tell Him to bless you, too.' He said okay, nodding his head. Then he turned and ran back to his mother, ecstatic since he had just solved all of my problems."

"Beautiful story," Sheleg said after a pause.

"Yes, and I'm telling it to you because something in your face reminds me of that little boy. Beyond the pity and compassion that some people feel for me, I saw a sincere expression of love in both of you," he said.

"So why did you let that ten-dollar bill go, giving it to the waiter?"

"I didn't let it go; I let myself go. My great punishment in life has been due to not sharing, and that's something we all must do, even when we mistakenly think we don't have anything left to share. Today I got to feel what that boy must have felt then, a genuine desire to give. I had that same feeling when, just as innocently as that boy had taken the bill out of his pocket, I took it out of mine," he explained.

Countless people hurried by on the sidewalk in front of them. Some totally ignored them, while others looked down at them as they rushed by. And some approached them and handed them money as they walked by.

"You can learn a lot from children and from the street. They are two great teachers," Sheleg observed.

"Sometimes you can learn even more than you would have liked," the old man replied. Then he asked, "You said you weren't from around here, right?"

"No, I'm not from here. I'm just visiting."

"Where do you live?"

"I grew up in Fiji," Sheleg answered.

"Fiji, eh? Where's that?"

Sheleg said, "It's on the other side of the ocean, very far away from here."

"I've only ever been to this city and the area around here, so I don't know where anything is. Is it pretty there?" the old man asked, curious.

"Yes, it's very beautiful. I grew up near the beach, in a place called Yasawa."

"Yasawa? How do you spell it?" he asked. "Couldn't you have grown up somewhere with an easier name?" He chuckled. "Okay, go on with your story."

"Yes, I grew up on that peninsula with my Papa Kamuela until I turned eighteen, and then I left with some friends of mine to go live in another country for a few years. We wanted to see other parts of the world and have some adventures at that point in our lives."

"I understand. And what about your mother?"

"I never knew her. And I never knew my real father, either. My Papa Kamuela raised me. He was sort of a stepfather."

"How did that affect you, never having known your parents?"

"It didn't really affect me that much, since where I grew up they have a whole different kind of family culture than here. There, everybody's a part of one big family. Your aunts are like mothers, cousins are like brothers and sisters, and when you reach a certain age, you become everyone's grandparent. So you can imagine, I had all the family you could ever dream of," Sheleg explained. "Even though I haven't seen them in a very long time, we're still very close. We lived together like a family, so I never felt deprived in that sense, and I love Papa Kamuela very deeply. He taught me what life is all about, and he's shared many of his secrets with me."

After a short pause, the old man, shaking his head, exclaimed, "Family! Bah! The only family I have is a stray dog who sleeps with me at night. I never had a family, and never will. That's my destiny."

"What does destiny mean to you?" Sheleg asked as a woman set down a paper bag in front of them, probably with some food in it.

"Destiny …?" he asked, contemplative. "I don't know. What do *I* know!" he shrugged. "Suffering, pain, loneliness, hunger, misery … any kind of bad luck you can think of."

"And when you look at somebody like that, what does destiny mean to you?" Sheleg asked, gesturing to a well-dressed passerby who looked like he had just left home after taking a nice shower.

The beggar studied the man and answered, "Envy, anger, failure … hopelessness … I don't know. I stopped thinking about that a long time ago." He was silent for a moment. "So why do you want to know, anyway?"

"Because everything you said is just how I would feel if I sat here watching all these successful people walk by, if I didn't have any hope of being successful, too," Sheleg said.

"You're very young to think that way, aren't you?"

"Yes, but life can be unfair whether you're young or old, and it can beat you down before you've even had a chance," Sheleg asserted, answering just like he figured the beggar would have if he had been asked.

"I think you're not appreciating everything you have!" the beggar said, taking Sheleg's bait.

"What I have? I don't have anything!" Sheleg said, still playing the beggar's role without the other man even realizing it.

"Well, look, you have two arms, two legs, a nose, a mouth. You have that shirt you're wearing, you have a bag with some money in it … look at everything you have inside you, and you'll see that you even have more than you need," the old man said, unwittingly saying the same things that people had always said to him, but he had refused to hear.

"I wish I was you; I'd rather be a beggar!" Sheleg said emphatically.

"No, son, this is no kind of life. Here on the street, life passes you by; people have abandoned you. Just look at me! Do you like what you see?"

"Of course I do! While some people are sleeping in five-star hotels enclosed in four concrete walls, you sleep under the star-studded sky. While other people are ruled by their work schedules and bosses, you spend your time however you want to; you don't have to answer to anybody. While some people have to decide what outfit to wear to make the right impression, you make an impression by your presence alone. That seems wonderful to me!" Sheleg explained.

"Well, let me tell you—you don't know what you're talking about, because I'm the most miserable man you can imagine, and nothing you've said makes any sense at all."

"And what if I offered to buy your life?" Sheleg asked. "Would you sell it to me?"

Puzzled, the old man replied, "What do you mean?"

"I'll give you all the money I have, all my possessions and property, and you give me everything you have. We'll trade places, and we'll see who's right. What do you think?"

"What are you talking about, boy! Have you gone crazy?"

"No, I'm serious. I'll give you absolutely everything I have, and you give me everything you have. What's so hard to understand about that?"

After a short silence, he answered, "Fine, I accept your offer. Give me your life and I'll give you mine. But I guarantee that you're going to regret it. At least I'll have more than I ever dreamed I'd ever have," the homeless man said.

"Okay, take it," Sheleg said, handing him his bag.

"Fine. And what about the rest?" he asked, shrugging his shoulders and holding out his arms.

"The rest of what?" Sheleg said.

"Money, possessions, properties ... everything you said you had!"

"I just gave you everything. That's all my property, all my possessions. There's nothing else; that's all I have," he said, showing his empty hands.

The beggar looked at him silently, then slowly he looked away and studied the ground, trying to decipher Sheleg's intentions. "I don't understand. What are you trying to do with this?" the homeless man asked, disconcerted.

"Since a minute ago, you're me and I'm you, so you should already know the answer to that question, since now we know each other equally well."

The beggar paused again and stroked his beard. Then he said, "I don't deserve your life, because you make beautiful things out of it. You know how to give, and how to receive, and I don't want to ruin what you've done with it," he concluded, absorbing the lesson.

"If you don't want to ruin it, then try and take care of it, because I'm not going to take it back. Now, I'm going to take your life and go all around the world with it, to see Fiji, and learn how to spell 'Yasawa'," Sheleg said.

Then all was silent. They didn't hear the traffic or the conversations of the people walking by. After looking off in every direction of the city, the old man said timidly, "Would you agree to something, if I asked for it with all my heart?"

"Yes, sir. Of course."

"I'll give you this bag back, in exchange for a hug," he said, smiling.

Sheleg smiled back, nodding. He tightly embraced the man he had shared a beautiful new experience with that afternoon. A few minutes later they said good-bye, each thankful for having had the opportunity to meet. And even though they probably would never meet again, they would always keep the memory of that moment, which had taught the older man that life will always give you a chance to change, under the strangest circumstances, when you least expect it.

CHAPTER 3

The dinner

"The mind is the link that joins
the soul with the body."

The nature of the soul is to give.
The nature of the body is to receive.
Conscience is the perfect balance between the two.

~ ~ ~

The evening at Jose and Mary's house unfolded pleasantly. Jose didn't have to go to work the next day, so the dinner was very relaxed.

"This is delicious!" Sheleg said.

"My grandmother taught me this recipe. She always made it for us when we were little; it was the only way she could get us to eat vegetables," Mary explained.

"It is really good. I have to admit, your grandmother really knew what she was doing in the kitchen," Jose said with a laugh.

"How long has it been since you stopped eating meat, Sheleg?" Mary asked.

"It's been fifteen years, ever since a trip to India."

"Did you stop eating it for any particular reason? Or just ..." Mary's voice trailed off.

"It's out of respect for animal life. They can nourish our spirits and our minds, if we only knew how to interact with them … and I witnessed first-hand how they suffer when they are slaughtered."

"But isn't it just part of the food chain?" Jose asked.

"I think that because we are beings of conscience, unlike animals, we are no longer a part of that food chain."

"Sure, but the fact is we have inherited certain eating habits genetically, and that translates into a need to consume certain things. And not only that, I understand that the human brain only began to evolve after we started eating meat," Mary commented, leaning back in her chair.

"As far as the development of the human brain, some theories hold that to be true," Sheleg answered. "But others assert that just at that point, a disequilibrium emerged because the evolutionary phase of the brain was much more accelerated than the evolution of the spirit. That's one of the reasons why there is such an imbalance between intellectual development and spiritual development. And as far as changing our eating habits, I agree with you. Everyone has to deliberately find the path that's right for them, and they have to consciously go about it. It would be very irresponsible to start changing a deep-set habit without first understanding how. We're talking about very gradual, integral processes which, if mismanaged, can end up hurting us more than helping us. In my own case, the process took several years. I gradually reduced the quantity of meat I ate and substituted other foods into my diet until I found my own balance. And I should point out that, very, very rarely, when my body asks for it, I eat fish or certain kinds of meat because of what you described, the 'genetic inheritance'."

"I think I see what you're getting at," Mary said.

Sheleg continued, "But above all, I think the most important thing is that we need to fundamentally change our attitude toward life. What's the point in just eating lettuce three times a day, if on the inside you're tearing your neighbor apart because hatred and envy are eating away at you?"

"Yes, of course," Jose said cheerfully, "that's what turns you into a kind of vegetarian-cannibal."

Sheleg laughed at this, as Mary smiled and added, "And you have to be very aware of the people around you. Sometimes we want to drag other people down through a personal decision of our own without considering that some people don't want to be involved in this. For example, one day a good friend of ours decided she was going to live on a macrobiotic diet and lifestyle. Just two months later she was on the brink of divorce, since she was driving her husband and the rest of the family crazy with all the weird things she was doing—things she didn't even understand herself."

"Hmmm! You must mean Estela, but she's been crazy for a long time," Jose added. "Every time she'd come over to visit, she'd bring a new philosophy of life with her, including all its accoutrements." Sheleg and Mary chuckled.

"Alright, but you know we always have a good time. And who are you to talk? You're the one who always says we should invite her over."

Jose laughed. "Okay, that's true. I admit it," he said, turning to look at Sheleg as he put a hand to his chest. "But you have to know this person and all her outlandish philosophies; she's a lot of fun. The other day she came over and told us about the 'prosperity fruit,' and can you believe she had me standing on my head in the middle of the living room, surrounded by apples with burning candles stuck in each one?"

Everybody laughed as Jose continued his story. "And the whole time my pant legs were slipping down! So for over ten minutes I had to put up with that and try to keep them from slipping all the way down, so that all the positive energy wouldn't escape. And she was reciting all these weird chants, and opening her hands! And then closing them!" He mimed the gestures. "I didn't know how I was going to get out of it, because she gets really offended if you say anything."

"She sure is a character," Mary laughed as she started clearing the table. "And her husband, Gregory, he must love her more than anything in the world. She can't exactly be the easiest person to live with."

"Yes," Jose nodded, "Gregory is the salt of the earth. If we have a chance I'd like to introduce you to him. Whenever something breaks around the house, he comes over and fixes it. No matter what it is, he can fix it. He's a great guy."

"Okay," Sheleg nodded, still chuckling over the scene with the apples and the candles.

"Should we go into the living room and open a bottle of wine?" Jose offered.

"Sounds good to me," Mary said.

"Yes, me too. And thanks so much for dinner," Sheleg said.

They had a wonderful time that evening, talking and laughing. Sheleg hadn't met Mary before. She was young, with straight, chestnut-colored hair, fair skin, and she was always flashing her lovely smile. Her eyes were jet black, in striking contrast with her hair. She was very self-assured, and she smoothly managed her professional life while running their home. Many of the works of art decorating her and Jose's home were her own creations, and she was slowly gaining local recognition for her work as an artist.

She and Jose had been married for three years, and even though they didn't have children, they were planning to have them soon. They balanced each other very well: he was very methodical and calculating, while she was very altruistic and esoteric. But they were very compatible; they really understood each other, which made them a very interesting couple in spite of their different approaches to life. She kept him on an even keel and helped him keep everything in perspective.

Mary had recently read a book about relationships and soul mates, and she was interested in hearing what Sheleg thought about the topic. He said, "When two soul mates meet, they should start to work together on something. One should complement the other, and they should both help each other to overcome their own limitations. In that way they will grow together, spiritually and intellectually, leaving no empty spaces between them."

"That seems logical, right? It's just common sense!" Jose exclaimed.

"Of course, that would be the logical approach. But then you find out that common sense is actually the most uncommon sense there is, and you're left with that sad paradox. Most of the time things don't happen like that. Over time, the relationship deteriorates because of a lack of communication, intolerance, and life's routine distractions, among other things, and in the end the neither person ever achieves their goals," Sheleg explained.

"So how do you think that can be avoided?" Mary asked.

"Well, you have to understand that each person's head is its own little world, and each world has its own story. While the primary factors in a relationship are always love and respect, there's another important ingredient that we eventually overlook, and that's communication. That love we feel at the beginning of a relationship often ends up getting shoved aside into a corner because of that silent syndrome, and then the misunderstandings and arguments begin. The silence leads, ultimately, to loneliness. Then we start to look for comfort in relationships outside of the marriage, and we share our feelings with friends and relatives instead of with our own spouses. We start to reinforce our own frustrations, and we end up detesting the person that we loved so much once."

"You know, that's what happened to Jose and me. At the beginning of our relationship, we let a lot of things slide. When we were still dating and newly in love, everything looked rosy, and we didn't worry about the little things. But as time passed, the little things seemed to get bigger and bigger, and we didn't know how to control them. What had been small, insignificant things were suddenly huge and intolerable. And the worst part is you don't want to talk about them with your partner, to avoid getting into a fight," Mary said while Jose settled into the sofa.

He added, "Luckily we understood what was really happening pretty fast—or really, Mary made *me* understand—and we decided that there weren't going to be any more secrets between us. If something came up for either one of us, we would tell each other right away and not let anything get out of control."

Jose leaned forward and picked up the bottle of wine, which he had been saving for this special occasion, and poured three glasses.

"I remember one thing that happened with Jose that completely changed our communication style," Mary went on. "I introduced him to a friend of mine from work. She's very pretty, and I could tell Jose was attracted to her. Later that night, instead of making a jealous scene and fighting about it, I just asked him to describe for me how he felt when he saw her. The question made him a little uncomfortable, and he tried to avoid answering. But I reminded him that we had promised to always be open and honest with each other and talk about things while they were still relatively unimportant, to make sure they didn't grow into real problems. I promised I wouldn't get mad if he was honest with me."

"So what happened?" Sheleg asked Jose, who was laughing as he remembered the incident.

"Well, I told her the truth. I said that as a man, I felt somehow attracted by her, and that I would have loved to have had the chance to sleep with the two of them at the same time. I said that that would have been better than winning the lottery for me."

"Then what did you say?" Sheleg asked Mary, smiling.

"I burst out laughing. What was I going to say? All men are the same; they only want one thing. But more than anything, honestly, it made me feel really good that he was able to open up to me because even if he hadn't told me, that wouldn't mean he wasn't still thinking about it. I'd rather he told me, so then what he's thinking becomes a part of me, too. That has really helped to strengthen our relationship."

"And let me say something," Jose cut in. "Ever since that day, I feel like Mary is my best friend, aside from being my wife, so I don't have to hide anything from her. You can't imagine how our relationship changed once we knew we could really express whatever we were feeling without having to be afraid that it might lead to a fight or confrontation."

"Yes, as long as you are always respectful and loyal to each other, everything works out," Mary added.

"What if Mary told you something like that? Would you react the same way as she did?" Sheleg asked Jose as he gazed at one of Mary's paintings, an abstract with maroon brushstrokes.

"I have to admit it was hard for me at first, but now, I would. Once Mary told me that one of her old boyfriends had called her up just to say hi. At first I felt really jealous and angry over what she might be feeling. But we talked about it, and I understand that we all have a past, and that past is just a part of our history. I know she loves me, and I love her. So instead of feeling threatened, I appreciated that she could share her experiences with me so we could get to know each other even better. I think the important thing is not to lose perspective on things and to know how to be really honest with each other."

"But getting back to soul mates, what else were you going to say?" Mary asked Sheleg.

He contemplated for a moment before giving his thoughts. "It's important to understand that the soul and energy are exactly the same thing; we shouldn't separate these concepts just because of semantics. The only difference is the context: theology uses the word 'soul' while science uses the word 'energy', but they are essentially the same thing," Sheleg explained.

"Soul mates come together in this physical plane to grow, work together, and reach a common goal together. Once their goal has been reached on this planet and in this life, in another dimension—after physical death—the two soul mates will fuse into one, becoming a single entity. And then this entity will reincarnate in this plane, on this planet, in a single body, but with a higher vibration as a result of the fusion of the soul-energies. And that's how the process starts all over again on this physical plane. The search for a soul mate begins anew, in this way creating more advanced, more highly evolved beings over time," Sheleg concluded.

"That's incredible," Mary commented.

"That's why we sometimes experience internal conflict that we don't even understand ourselves," Sheleg rationalized. "It's because these energies inside us that were at one time independent are now joined together as one"

"What happens after that? After the merged souls are reincarnated?" Jose asked, fascinated.

"As I started to say, the process of soul unification goes on repeating itself. We keep on growing and evolving, one lifetime after another. And it doesn't just happen with our spouses, because you can also join your soul with other people if you have come to understand each other at a very deep, profound level."

"According to what you're saying, I would imagine that after thousands of years we could reach levels of energy and conscience almost beyond our comprehension, right?" Mary asked.

"That's the idea, to keep on growing and developing mentally and spiritually. Remember that we currently only use something like five percent of our brains. With this evolution we'll gradually increase that capacity until some time in the future, we'll use one hundred percent."

"So what we see today is just the tip of the iceberg in terms of human development?" Jose asked thoughtfully, leaning forward on the sofa and clasping his hands together.

"Exactly. Just imagine the force of energy we'll emanate someday. The time will even come when our bodies will no longer be what they are now, and that will happen as a part of this evolutionary process. Just think what will happen when, in the distant future, all of the souls will finally be merged into one. The earth will transform into a new sun, which will in turn give life to a new planet, and the whole evolutionary process will start over from the beginning, just as happened on our planet at one time."

"Do you mean that our sun was once what the earth is now?" Jose asked, turning his head.

"It's one theory ..."

Mary slipped her shoes off and crossed her feet on the sofa she shared with Jose, as he asked, "That's really interesting. Let me ask you something. How do you know all that fused energy won't be used for something bad?"

"In order to fuse together, souls have to reach a certain level first. They can find each other and share a life on this planet, but they can't fuse together unless they reach their objective here. As long as they don't, they'll keep on being reincarnated as individual energies until finally they can fuse."

"My God! There must be so many people being recycled for all eternity on this planet," Jose exclaimed, thinking about his divorced parents, who were always fighting even though deep down they couldn't live without each other. "These souls will have to live life after life together until they finally decide to get along." Everyone laughed at this.

Outside, as the night wore on, the temperature continued to drop on this early spring evening. But Sheleg, Jose, and Mary were completely removed from the chill, as several logs burning in the fireplace suffused the room with a cozy warmth.

"So what happens to the souls that instead of evolving only hurt others, like a rapist, a killer, or a dictator?" Mary asked.

"In that case, the process is reversed; the soul fragments and reincarnates in different people, diluting its energy levels and forming groups—like, for instance, families or social circles—and they'll have to figure out how to start the process of reunification again. These groups usually pay the consequences for their actions in very unfavorable life conditions," Sheleg explained. "For example, they say that for people who take the lives of others, one fragmentation results for each victim. And each fragmentation, or the soul each such person, 'pays' in direct proportion to the suffering that the person caused in his past life, in this way forming an equilibrium of energy that will finally create a conscience in that person."

There was a short silence as Mary and Jose seemed to absorb this.

"Is this theory you're talking about what you'd call Karma?" Jose asked.

"You could say that. It's part of a process via which we create ourselves through our actions. We came here to make up for any past suffering we may have caused, with the ultimate goal of reaching a state of perfection as human beings."

"It's an interesting theory. It explains why there's so much injustice in the world," Mary said as she twisted her hair. "But these ideas hard to accept because you can't see the reasons behind them."

"It's a matter of opening your mind and seeing how evolution has affected all species. Just imagine millions of years ago, when we were all just single-cell microorganisms: could you ever have thought then that someday there would be laptop computers, the Internet, and jet planes flying all around the skies?" Sheleg asked.

"Yes, you're right," Jose interjected. "Over time, even the most outlandish ideas eventually become routine."

"Does your wife Michelle share these views?" asked Mary.

"We came up with most of them together. We have long conversations, and these ideas come to us. When we get stuck on something, usually answers will come over time."

"And how do the answers come to you?" Jose asked.

"Through a book that we come across, or from talking with people, observing things that happen in life … or sometimes a really clear idea will just come to you, as if you had an antenna growing out of your head and you could receive the answers. It's like when you come up with an idea that seemed to just come out of nowhere."

"I know what you mean," Jose jumped in. "That happens to me a lot; I don't know how to solve a problem … and *bam*! the solution just comes."

"That's because everything has an answer, and that answer can be found in the empty space between you and I, in that dimension we can't see," Sheleg explained.

"So if all the answers are already someplace, all you have to come up with is the questions?" Mary asked.

"Exactly!"

"How do you turn on those antennas?" Jose asked, half-jokingly.

Sheleg answered seriously, "Through something known as the sixth sense, or intuition."

"Do we all have it?" Jose asked.

"Of course. You just said yourself that sometimes ideas just come to you out of nowhere. That is the sixth sense, and we all have it. We just need to develop it—to consciously work on it, taking the time to sit with ourselves and explore everything that's inside of each one of us."

"I understand," Jose said. Then after a lull in the conversation, he changed the subject. "So I guess Michelle decided not to come with you? She stayed at home?"

"Yes. We usually travel together, but this time she wanted to stay in Papua. Like I said on the phone, she's four months pregnant, and she also wanted to finish up a project we've been working on."

"What kind of project?" Mary asked.

"We're spending some time there in an indigenous village, learning how to use natural medicines to cure terminal illnesses. Michelle believes that certain techniques could complement what she knows about pharmacology and that she could make some important advances in the field," Sheleg explained.

"She's studied pharmacology?" inquired Mary.

"Yes, she got a degree in pharmacology from the University of Valparaiso in Chile."

"Oh," Jose said, "is she Chilean?"

"No, she's European, but she grew up in South America. Her parents are diplomats, and they were assigned there while she was a teenager."

Jose asked, "How long have you known each other?"

Sheleg paused to recollect. "Let's see, I guess we've known each other for almost fourteen years now. We met in Botswana, in southern Africa. She was working on a project for her thesis, and I was exploring that part of the world. We've been together ever since," Sheleg said, smiling.

"You really have seen the world!" Jose said with a laugh. "I spend my whole life working like a dog, and if I'm lucky I take one vacation a year, while you haven't stopped traveling around the whole planet, trying to find yourself in the farthest corners of the earth."

They all laughed at Jose's insight since, as paradoxical as it seemed, it was true.

"Well, it's not as simple as it sounds. These trips were often to places where children die of malnutrition every day, or they involved traveling to very inhospitable environments after a natural disaster, or even being caught in the crossfire at places we were going to teach … we have so many stories that are beyond description. But they haven't been easy, even though we have learned so much from them."

"I see," Jose said, realizing that "travel" doesn't always mean "vacation."

Mary asked, "So what are your plans now that you're going to have a child?"

"We're going to South Africa, to the outskirts of Cape Town. We're going to work on a project called Eco-Universities. A local group there called Glean started it a few years ago. The program gives free classes on ecology and conservation to low-income people."

"Oh, really?" Jose said.

"Yes. The idea is that once the students graduate from the program and they're out in the work force, they'll apply what they've learned on projects that will allow sustainable development without having a negative impact on the planet, no matter what their specific profession. For example, if you want to study auto mechanics, you would work on creating affordable cars that don't harm the environment. If you're studying economics, you would work on developing economic models that would be free of worker exploitation. If you study urban development, you would try and create cities that have only a minimal impact on the environment. The overall idea is to apply what you've learned in a productive way, adapting to our current reality in a harmonious way."

"That is really fascinating," Jose said.

"It is, and it's been going really well. When the program first started, Eco-Universities was housed in a really old building out in the countryside with just fifteen students and one teacher. Now, they have three centers and over seven hundred students."

"So what are you two going to do there?" Mary asked.

"At first I'm going to give classes in systems, which is my specialty, and Michelle's going to work in their new pharmacology department. In the near term, the goal is to keep on expanding the program, hiring more teachers, and developing a solid structure to be able to then expand to other locations."

"Where does the funding come from?"

"Right now, mostly from grants from the South African government and private foundations. But the organization is trying to become financially independent, using a model developed by one of the professors where graduates of the program would pay for the new students."

"It's really interesting. Everything you're doing is wonderful; you can count on our support for anything you need," Jose said.

"Thank you. It's a very important project. Education is crucial for everybody, especially when it helps us understand how we should be doing things in general. And it's very important to eradicate ignorance, which is one of the worst things there is in society and the world at large."

"That's great. And what else have you done around the world?" Mary asked.

"Well, recently Michelle's been working on the project in Papua as I told you. Over the past two years before that, Michelle and I worked at the University of Ottagaha in New Zealand with a group of scientists who are researching how mind and matter are related. It all started when 'by chance'—" Sheleg made the gesture for air quotes, "—we met an uncle of a friend of mine, who teaches cognitive sciences at that university. He wanted us to work on a new project the university had decided to fund. I developed several statistical programs with another student, while Michelle worked on scientific research with some another group."

"So did you live at the university?" Mary asked.

"Yes, at that time we were guests of the university, until the project in Papua came up, where we are now. But the main thing is we don't do it to make money or just to have a job. We do it because we think it's important to work for change and raising of awareness overall. Just from this desire to do these things, opportunities just seem to come up on their own."

"It's all very interesting," Jose said. "So it seems there's an institutional involvement behind all this, right?"

"There is a great deal of interest in energy, the mind, and the spirit in many research labs and institutions now, and it's growing. And that has opened doors for us, because aside from our interest in the subject, we also have strong backgrounds. That's why we believe so strongly in the importance of education, and we want to help move this project in South Africa forward."

"Well, that's wonderful," Mary said. "I'm sure you have a lot of fascinating stories to tell."

"Oh, I sure do. Here, let me give you an example of how things can sometimes unfold and you get what you need without even having to ask," Sheleg related. "Once while we were in that country, a group of villagers had to go to Port Moresby, the capital of Papua New Guinea. Michelle and I decided to go with them to see the city. While we were having lunch in a little café, we started talking to the waiter, and he told us about how the owner of the place was going through a really rough time. His daughter was very sick with a virus, and the doctors thought her chances of survival were very slim. We told the waiter that Michelle had a background in medicine and that I had experience using the hands' energy to heal, and if the girl's father wanted, we would try to help her.

"The waiter got in touch with his boss, and he asked us to go to his house. The waiter took us there himself, where we met the girl, who was around twelve years old. They told us we could stay in their house for as long as we needed, and then we got to work trying to help her."

"Where did you learn about healing with your hands?" Jose asked, intrigued.

"In New Zealand, at a healing center … the things you can learn there are so interesting—"

Jose interrupted, "And what is it, exactly, healing with your hands? What did you do to try and cure the girl?"

"Well," Sheleg started, "It's different with each person. In this case, the first time I walked into the girl's room, I remember she was lying in bed with the saddest look, complaining of pain. I said hello and asked if I could sit down next to her. I took her hand in mine and listened to her. I didn't say a word, and a minute later, she closed her eyes and fell asleep. In the silence, an image came into my mind of the affected area, and her grandmother's absence, the coldness she felt when she thought about her brother—who she hadn't seen in years—and the countless needle jabs she had endured from so many shots she had been given, and the silenced scream in her heart."

"She transmitted all of those feelings to you?" Mary asked, incredulous.

"She allowed it to happen. It all depends on the person who needs help, and how much they want to be healed."

"That's amazing," Mary said.

"Yes, really amazing," Jose agreed. "And I have some little aches and pains you could help me out with, any time …"

"Of course," Sheleg said, grinning.

"But tell me more about the healing. Was that transition of feelings all? Why is it through the hands?" Jose asked.

"No, Jose; Michelle played a role, too. As for the hands, they are a vehicle for giving and receiving—and not just material things, but energy, too."

"I see."

"So what happened with the girl?" Mary asked.

"Michelle prepared several special medicines for her, together with their family doctor. A few days later, she started to get better. Her fever subsided, and gradually she got stronger and stronger."

"What a blessing. I can just imagine how grateful the family was," Mary said.

"Yes, it was one of the most beautiful experiences we've ever had. The family cried from happiness every time they remembered how the little girl had gotten better. Before we left, they threw a party for us, and they even invited some people from the neighborhood. The girl's father gave us an envelope and said we should do what we thought was best with what was inside it. There was almost twenty thousand dollars in it. He told is it was the amount he had saved up to take his daughter to Scotland for a special treatment. That amount of money was a fortune in that country, so we decided to donate ten thousand to a research institution that was trying to eradicate malaria. We saved the rest for the future. We're still using some of that money to live on quite comfortably, and we shared some of it with the poor people from the area," Sheleg concluded.

"I'm so impressed with everything you're doing, Sheleg. Life has taken you to some incredible places … and you still haven't told us why you came here. What do you have to do here that's so important and that has something to do with me?" Jose asked.

Sheleg leaned forward and started to explain. "Over the last few weeks, your name has popped into my head many times. When something like that happens, I'm very aware of the signs that tell me where the thought is coming from. I felt it was very important that I get in touch with you, so I did. After we first got back in touch, I felt an incredibly strong impulse to come here, so I meditated, asking for a clear sign to come to me of whether I should come or not. The next day, very early in the morning, Michelle asked me to pick up a few things at the grocery store. I went and bought what she had asked for. The man at the counter wrapped my purchases in a page from an English-language newspaper. This was very unusual, since newspapers almost never even reach that village, much less in English," Sheleg said.

"Uh-huh." Mary and Jose both nodded.

"When I got home, I opened up the newspaper and saw an ad for an airline that said, 'Come to the Big Apple, wonderful surprises await you.'"

"You're kidding! Only the day before you asked for a sign to see if you should come to New York or not, and then you saw that ad. What a coincidence!" Mary exclaimed.

"Yes, and I still have that page from the newspaper; I saved it," Sheleg said as he searched for the page in his bag. "And the most impressive thing of all is the price they advertised for the ticket," he added as he took the newspaper page out of his bag.

"It's \$333, round-trip," Mary said, not understanding the significance of this number.

"To make a long story short, many years ago, while I was in a deep state of meditation at a Mayan ruin site in Guatemala, that number was revealed to me. It appeared in my mind in a deep blue color. And ever since then, every time it pops up, it's a sign that my life is in sync—that I'm on the right path," Sheleg explained.

"And that very number was the price of the ticket. Aside from the ad advertising the Big Apple … and in a newspaper that came from who knows where … too many coincidences to ignore, isn't it?"

"Exactly."

"But isn't it kind of risky to base decisions in those kinds of situations on factors that could be just circumstantial?" Jose asked.

"After many experiences, you discover that nothing is just

circumstantial. First, when you let your intuition, which inspires you to do things, be your guide, you learn that these kinds of coincidences only confirm your intuition."

"So when you tell people all this, do they believe you?" Jose asked.

"It's not a question of whether people believe me or not, because I'm not trying to convince anybody of anything. The point is, everyone has access to this connection with life. It's just a matter of wanting to do it."

"So, if somebody wanted you to prove to them that it worked, could you?" Jose asked, showing a bit of skepticism.

"The best proof is for everybody to discover it for themselves," Sheleg countered. "The idea is for each person to understand their own reality, and not just blindly follow somebody else's ideas."

"Then tell me, how do you connect with this internal world, with intuition and everything you're talking about?" Jose asked.

Sheleg replied, "I can teach you how to do it little by little, starting with the most basic techniques, and gradually you'll develop your own techniques."

"I'm all ears," Jose said, looking at Mary.

"Alright. Let's do a meditation, and as we go along, I'll explain everything. The most important thing is to reach a very positive mental state and to have an open mind, okay?" Sheleg said. He reached into his bag and took out a CD. "Here, play this."

Jose took the CD sleeve in his hands and set it down on the table. He turned it over, frowning, and then placed it next to an envelope that he had brought home from the office that day. "Look, what a coincidence," he said. "This envelope I brought home from the office has the same signature as the one on Sheleg's CD."

"What?" Sheleg said curiously as Jose handed it to him.

"How interesting. The security guard at your building signed this for me before I went up to your office this morning," Sheleg explained.

"And the same guard gave this envelope to me. Now I understand. I thought some kind of witchcraft was going on in this house. I picked it up just a few minutes before we met up to come here together," Jose said.

Sheleg recalled how Terry, the security guard, was having trouble signing the CD sleeve, and he had tried to sign the blank white envelope that was on the counter. Apparently it was the same envelope that Jose now held in his hands.

"Of course! Now I understand all this," Sheleg said. He told them the autograph story.

"Well, it's just a coincidence," Jose said after Sheleg finished.

"I don't think so … there must be something more to it. It seems like a pretty big coincidence that he signed two autographs, and now I have one and you have the other."

"But come on! Does there always have to be something more behind everything with you? It's just a coincidence, and that's it," Jose said, chuckling.

"Do you really think so?" Mary asked, interested to hear Sheleg's explanation.

"I don't know," he said thoughtfully. "What's in that envelope?"

"Wait, let me open it." After reading it, he said, "It's an invitation from my friend Desmond. He's a music producer, and his record label is having a record-release party."

"*Ha*!" Sheleg laughed. "You have no idea what this means!" Then he told them about the conversation he had had with the guard that morning.

"Wow, will you look at that?" Mary said after Sheleg finished the story. "The same guard who's trying to get his musical career off the ground talks to you, signs an envelope from a record producer who's also a friend of Jose's … and all this happens … that's a lot of coincidences for one day."

"You're right … you've even convinced me," Jose added, smiling.

"Why don't you talk to Desmond and tell him about this guy, Terry, and see if he can do anything to help him?" Mary asked.

Jose nodded assent. "If he plays at the Big Jazz, he's got to be good; they don't let just anybody play there."

"I heard part of one of his songs while were talking, and it was really good," Sheleg confirmed. "And he's definitely got charisma. He's a really nice guy."

"No problem, then. Tomorrow I'll call up Desmond and I'll have him come over to the office on Monday. We can have a coffee and he can meet Terry."

"Isn't it incredible how things work out!" Mary exclaimed.

"Yes, it really was quite a coincidence," Jose conceded.

"Now do you see how everything that happens, happens for a reason?" Sheleg chided Jose.

"Alright, alright! Sometimes these things happen, it's true … but let's get back to that meditation we were going to do. I'll put on this record," he said as he went over to the CD player.

"I'm going to light some candles and incense," Mary said.

Some very soothing music gently filled the room; the tune consisted of flutes that sounded very far away. The relaxing music perfectly complemented the soft candlelight and the fire in the fireplace that infused the room with warmth.

All was peaceful, and the night's silence seemed to speak to them. Outside, a fine mist gently fell on the tulips, and a soft breeze rustled over the treetops. In the distance, crickets chirped, making that special sound that belongs to the night. Inside, the soothing music settled into the room, while the scent of the forest wafted in through a cracked window as the brisk air from the night's passing cold front greeted them.

"Sit down comfortably and close your eyes," Sheleg instructed. "Try to eliminate any negative feelings you may have. In your mind, envision a planet, a country, a home—whatever you want—and ask the universe to give you what you've always wanted, and see that in your mind's eye. Ask the universe to answer a question that has no answer, and work with that internal voice inside of you. Vow to make the best use you can of whatever information comes to you."

The three were sitting on the floor with their eyes closed, each transported away by their own thoughts.

The minutes passed. Jose, who had been the most skeptical, seemed to be connecting on a much deeper level than Sheleg and Mary would have thought possible for him. He was submerged in himself, and even though he lost his concentration at times, he was able to regain it. That is, until finally he said out loud, "I have a problem."

"What is it?" Sheleg asked, eyes still shut.

"A client who I can't stand keeps popping into my head, and he's dragging me off of my celestial path," Jose said wryly, his eyes still closed.

"Fine, now try to identify what exactly about him bothers you so much. Imagine that the two of you are together somewhere talking. Immerse yourself in the conversation. Don't try to control it; just let him talk, and listen to what he has to say."

"Okay," he said, adjusting his posture.

Sheleg added, "Try and see him as a friend. Make him a part of you, and try to find a real desire for understanding."

"Alright," Jose said, continuing with his meditation.

Almost twenty minutes passed as the three sat unmoving on the floor with their eyes closed, not saying a word. Jose breathed slowly and seemed very comfortable with himself. The soft music flowed through the room, and the flickering of the candlelight seemed to be in sync with the melody's rhythm. They were each fully immersed in their own experience, in their own world. Finally, Jose let out a long sigh and opened his eyes gradually as he grew accustomed to the candlelight. Mary and Sheleg looked at him and smiled, since he had been in that peaceful state for a long time. They hadn't expected the skeptic to stick with the meditation as long as they had.

"*Wow*! If I hadn't experienced it for myself, I never would have believed it," Jose started to explain. "I listened to that internal voice you were talking about. It's hard to explain, but I was really connected with something that gave me an incredibly peaceful feeling. I sensed that you two were there … and I sensed that client I was telling you about. I did what you said, Sheleg. I sat down with him in a park and talked to him. I began to understand why he is the way he is, and I felt bad about having judged him. I came to understand that he had a reason for doing things the way he did, and that we all have a history that marks us and makes us who we are. I even saw that many of the things about him that I rejected were also characteristics of myself, and that his faults were a reflection of my own," Jose finished.

Surprised, Sheleg replied, "You've made very fast progress; usually people aren't able to visualize so many things at first … that's great! Now you can see that the defects we see in other people are just a reflection of our own. That's one more way that the universe communicates with us, so we need to learn to be consciously aware of it."

"So why is it so hard to see our own flaws?" Mary wondered aloud.

"Our egos usually don't allow us to recognize them. That's why life is always putting us into situations with the kind of people that bother us so much. This is the universe loudly pointing out to us everything we need to correct in our own behavior, and until we do, our lives will keep on repeating those kinds of situations, with those kinds of people," Sheleg observed.

"Yes, I see. Even just after the experience I just had, I understand a little better why you say something was pulling you to come here. If I could feel all of these things just in a few minutes, I can imagine what you'd feel after so many years of lighting candles and listening to those flutes," Jose said lightly.

Mary laughed at her husband's comment. She was still astonished, since she had never thought she would ever see him in such a spiritually receptive state.

"The main thing is to always keep our thoughts and feelings positive," Sheleg said, "since that is the only way to clearly see the situations in our lives and identify our options. Otherwise, the ego takes control, making us believe that we're victims and making us blame everyone around us, thus falsely releasing us from our responsibilities."

"So we need to repress the ego," Mary commented.

"That's just it, since the ego is our only real enemy. The ego is that noise in the background that prevents us from hearing the voice of our conscience; it's that little pest that tells us we're right and the rest of the world is wrong. It's what makes us explode with anger and act without thinking. We have to constantly keep our egos in check so we can really be at peace and see life more clearly, with the inner light that we can all generate ourselves."

"How do we do that?" Jose asked.

"First, by simply recognizing that it exists, because the most effective weapon the ego has is making us believe that this light doesn't exist. The ego's other weapon is our belief that it can't control us. But when we understand that the ego is only a part of us and is always ready to confuse us, then we can better manage situations. Second, we can't allow any negative thoughts or feelings to take root in us. And third, we can't react impulsively over anything, since even though that kind of response can feel very satisfying in the short term, it will cause serious problems over the long term."

"But that's not easy to do at all," Jose said, "since constantly the dynamic of life makes you feel upset or angry about almost anything."

"That's true. But if you are aware of the fact that we all create what happens in our lives, it's easier to manage, because then *you* are solely responsible for the situation, and then you can assume the consequences."

"How's that?" Jose asked. "Do you mean that if I'm here sitting in this chair and suddenly the lamp falls on my head, that's my fault?"

"Exactly, since it's the result of your past attitudes, actions, or behaviors, manifesting in this. It's called cause and effect."

"Okay … and what can I do so it doesn't happen to me anymore?" Jose asked.

"The same way—by taking control of your mind, eliminating negativity, and repressing the ego's impulses. If you do these things you'll see how your life will gradually become more orderly, and the chaos in your life will slowly disappear," Sheleg said. "When something disagreeable happens to you, don't get upset. Don't feel like a victim of circumstance, and don't give in to your initial impulse to explode in a fury. Instead, stay calm, relax, and try to come up with a solution. By calmly, consciously facing obstacles, you'll be able to end negative cycles and, in a way, close out old debts. But if you thoughtlessly act out of frustration and anger, you're only creating new cycles that perpetuate the chaos and confusion in your life."

The night had been a very unusual one for Jose and Mary. Time had passed quickly. It was almost dawn, and the three went to bed, very tired. The music, the candlelight, and the burning incense awaited daybreak, keeping whatever it was that had compelled Sheleg to come to New York.

CHAPTER 4

Questions and answers for Jose

"Life gives us challenges;
we put obstacles in our way."

Love is an outlook
that lets you be in perfect
harmony and balance with the universe
and teaches you the difference between
challenges and obstacles.

~ ~ ~

Jose was standing in a crowded subway car. This was not a normal event, since he usually was driven to work in a limousine or drove himself in his own car, but things had changed ever since he had seen Sheleg again. Several days had passed since their dinner and night of conversation, and everything seemed to be enveloped in some very interesting energies.

For Jose, venturing into his own inner world was something completely new. At first, he had maintained a certain level of skepticism about everything Sheleg was talking about: love, instincts, seeing the signs—but it was no less true that his friend's presence signified a very positive change and prompted him to view life from another perspective. It was as if he simply couldn't resist the change—something was making him listen to his friend and follow his teachings. By eliminating negativity, prejudice, anger, fear, dependence, hatred, and anger, he was making room to cultivate other, more important values. He felt strong and full of energy, which made sense because he was no longer wasting his time with senseless arguing or blaming other people for his problems.

Now he spent more time on his personal life, with Mary, and even with his own employees. He was much calmer about everything: a red light was not a signal that he would be late for work, but rather a signal that there was no rush; leaving his cell phone on his desk before he went out for lunch wasn't a tragedy, but a sign that he should just relax and have a nice meal, and, in general, if something didn't work out as expected, he viewed the result as being better that way anyway. So Jose, a scrupulous analyst of every move he made, stopped getting bogged down in irrelevant, time-consuming details; he simply watched his life unfold in front of him, enjoying it just as if it were a movie directed by a higher power.

He recalled something he had read in the book recently:

> Don't regret the past; live in the present. And don't be afraid of the future, because life is what is happening in this very minute. The future will come at just the right time.

So there Jose was in that crowded subway car, putting everything he had been learning to the test. He remembered how the previous night, before he had gone to sleep, he had asked life a few questions: *How do I know if I'm going down the right path? How do I know this isn't all a big lie? How can I be sure this isn't just some passing thing that Sheleg brought out in me? Please, answer me …*

Two stops before he was going to get off the train, a man across the aisle stood up and departed, leaving behind a newspaper. Jose picked it up and tried to give it back to the man, but it was too late; the doors closed. He stood in the middle of the car clutching a newspaper that wasn't his, unsure of how this type of situation was usually handled in a New York subway. He laughed to himself and thought, *Maybe this newspaper is destined to be mine*!

When the subway doors opened at his station, he headed for the north exit, the one closest to his office building. Without knowing why, he stopped and opened up the newspaper at random. There was a full-page ad, which said:

> *You'll know you're headed in the right direction when you see me.*
>
> In the center of the page was a large circle with three numbers in it:

555

Jose was puzzled. It was an ad for a new highway that was just opening outside of the city, called Highway 555. But for him, the ad had another meaning. Just the night before he had asked for a sign that he was on the right path, and now he felt that the answer was coming to him through this advertisement …

After a few minutes, he smiled, remembering how Sheleg had told him about his personal experience with the number 333. From now on, he decided, he knew that every time he saw the number 555 was a clear sign that he was headed in the right direction.

His smile broadened as he climbed the stairs out of the subway. He was experiencing for himself the phenomenon of seeing life's signs and following his own intuition. He was beginning to feel that constant, strange connection that Sheleg told him he (and everyone) had with the universe. Jose was dazzled by it, and he knew he could not let any negative thoughts or doubts creep in, trying to convince him that it was nothing more than coincidence. He remembered what Sheleg had said when they'd discussed some things the day before: "The secret is to always hold on to that state of mental and spiritual purity; otherwise reality will see you through some very long, chaotic journeys."

Jose was relaxed. He had been in a "pure" state for several days, free of negative or unhealthy thoughts, guaranteeing, in his mind, that everything was his under control. And even though his innate skepticism flared up now and then, he had learned how to quickly repress it.

Seeing George Bush's face on TV without getting angry or irritable was his litmus test. "The clearest sign of my self-control," he joked to himself. Usually just the sight of the president put him in a very foul mood, prompting him to get up, change the channel, or start yelling at the television, unleashing his anger at the man who, in his mind, was supposedly to blame for a great many things. But lately that hadn't been the case. He no longer felt the same irrational anger against that person. Now he viewed him calmly and, most surprisingly, even with affection. Sometimes in his meditations Jose pictured them both talking about international politics and spirituality in a café in the center of Baghdad. Through this Jose started to understand that we are all part of the same collective and that together and united we can make real, meaningful changes.

That isn't to say Jose didn't ever have his doubts about Sheleg's way of seeing the world. *Could Sheleg be a spy for the Republican party, sent here to brainwash me and make me send a big donation to his party?* Jose mused. *Well, the truth is he doesn't even believe in political parties, or even in many kinds of "leaders." so I don't have to worry about that*, he concluded. Besides, Sheleg had said before that he would never let his own life's destiny be controlled by anyone other than himself, so he didn't lay his ambitions, dreams, or goals onto other people's shoulders. These thoughts reassured Jose once more.

As he walked into his office building, he remembered something somebody had said once: "Even though I understand and respect the importance of nationalities, religions, and governments, I don't really feel represented by any of them; we belong to something bigger than a nation demarked by human boundaries. Our religion should be love, because it unites without discriminating; and our government should be our own conscience, since it is what really can connect us to the truth."

The elevator he had taken up to his floor opened and he got off, waving good-bye to those who were continuing on to a higher floor. He nodded hello to Jennifer, who was on the phone. He walked down the long hallway and went into his office, where a huge pile of papers he needed to review awaited him. Usually Jose would open every file and carefully read through every piece of paper, but now he felt that everything in life was in order, and maybe he could give his approval of the stack of documents without getting too involved in every little detail.

Will that be the right choice? his conscience asked him. He stood at the door looking at the files as he instinctively turned on the television—something he hadn't done for days, since he felt that his old addiction to the news and following the stock market had been consuming too much of his thoughts and energy. He looked out the window, into the blue sky, and asked, "Tell me, God, do you think it would be worth it for me to look through every single file here?"

Just then Joanne walked in and said with a smile, "Good morning, how are—?" She didn't finish. Then she asked, "What's that smell?"

"Incense," Jose said bashfully, a bit embarrassed. "I lit some last night before I went home. Do you like it?" he asked rapidly, hoping for her approval.

"Of course I do; I just never would have guessed that someday you would decide to join the human race," she teased.

"Well, I'm not such a monster, am I?" he replied.

"No, not a monster … just a grouch with neurotic tendencies."

Jose looked at her circumspectly and asked seriously, "Do you really mean that?"

She said, "Jose, you're like a son to me, you know that. And lately I've noticed that you're much calmer. The atmosphere in the whole office has really changed in the last few days, and that's really good. But you know very well that you generally tend to lose perspective, and you can create a really hostile vibe in the office. So just keep doing whatever you're doing, because you feel really good, and everybody else does, too … I think you're already seeing the results."

"Yes, you're right; I have noticed a change around the office. It's made me realize how many things I was doing wrong around here, and I'm trying to correct them … thank you. What would I do without you!" he exclaimed, surprising her with a warm hug.

"You really are changing, my boy," she said, raising an eyebrow and swatting his arm playfully. "And can I take these files out of here?"

Jose turned toward his desk as he heard an ad on the television: "Take advantage of Romino's Pizza's special 555 offer!"

He smiled and said to Joanne, "Yes, you can take them; they're approved."

"That's a miracle," she murmured as she quickly moved to take the pile of files before Jose changed his mind.

That number was beginning to manifest itself in Jose's life, and it made him feel sure that the steps he was taking were heading him in the right direction.

IIIIIIIIIII

And so the days passed. Everything was going just fine in Jose's life; nothing upset him, he was never in a rush, and he was in rhythm and generally happy. At the office he was at peace, and everything moved along without too much effort or delay. Jose was radiating something that was gradually spreading out and touching more and more people around him. It was very hard to explain, but very easy to feel.

One night Jose arrived home late after an unusually long day at work. Everyone was asleep. Lying in bed, he looked up at the ceiling, thinking about everything that was happening to him. He couldn't fall asleep, and he felt such a strong impulse to do something that he quietly got out of bed without waking Mary, went over to the bookcase in their bedroom, and in the darkness pulled out a book at random. He quietly left the bedroom and went into the den, where he lit a large candle and sat down on the loveseat. He started reading the page he happened to open to:

IIIIIIIIIII

Palden Lhamo could be one of the ugliest creatures in the cosmos. Her image, displayed in countless homes and temples, so frightened the first Western visitors to Tibet that they decided to call her "The Great Devil."

But it hadn't always been that way. Palden Lhamo, which meant "Glorious Goddess," had at first been the most beautiful woman on earth. Every man, every god, begged her to be his queen. Finally she consented to the most respected king, who ruled a noble, prosperous area of Southern India.

But things were gradually changing in the kingdom, and to ensure the empire's continued prosperity, once a year the king ordered that a perfect child be sacrificed. "If this sacrifice will ensure that the disease, war, and poverty that we see in other lands stays far away from here, then fine, one child less," the king proclaimed.

On the afternoon of one of these dreaded ceremonies, Palden Lhamo said to him, "You must put an end to this shameful ritual. I am a mother, and I know how a mother feels when she loses her child."

"Don't tell me how to rule my kingdom," the king replied irritably, "and don't forget that this ritual has brought you many benefits as well."

"You must stop it right now, or you will lose me forever!" she yelled.

Ignoring her, the king gave the order for the ceremony to continue, so the beautiful queen decided to put one of her sons on the sacrificial altar instead of the innocent child that was about to be sacrificed.

"Have you gone mad!" the king screamed. "That's my precious son." He took him by the arm and pulled him to one side, while he ordered that the ritual continue with the boy who had been originally chosen.

"Don't you understand that every child is a precious treasure to someone?" Palden Lhamo said desperately, the gaze of her indigo eyes intensifying. "Every mother grieving because of your actions will be weeping for all eternity. Please, have mercy on them!" But her words were in vain, and the ritual continued.

Peace and prosperity reigned for another year throughout the kingdom, and when the year was up, it was time for another sacrifice. Once again, Palden Lhamo put one of her own children on the sacrificial altar, but once again the king intervened, putting another child in his place with no intention of changing the cruel destiny that awaited him. So a third year came, and Palden Lhamo failed once again to convince the king to stop the ritual.

Her increasing desperation and powerlessness made her completely unhinged, until one day she decided to sacrifice her own two sons herself, without telling the king. When the king found out about what had happened, he was devastated. Finally, out of his own pain and suffering, he abolished the hateful ritual forever. But by then it was too late, since Palden Lhamo had plunged into madness and grown increasingly disconnected from reality. She decided to flee the kingdom forever, running away from the man she no longer loved, who had brought her to do such a horrible thing.

Her exquisite beauty traveled with her, compelling men and gods to ask for her hand, until the king of demons took her away with him, down to his dark world. Palden Lhamo spent years in the awful kingdom of cruelty ruled by the demon, until one night she decided to steal his sword and his coat of diseases, and escaped back to earth.

She vowed that her beauty would never again bring her to ruin, so she destroyed it … her clothes became disheveled rags, her skin grew blackened with filth, her nails grew like daggers, and her hair became a wild, snarled mess. Since she hardly ever ate, her perfect curves were reduced to sharp, skeletal angles.

It was all according to Palden Lhamo's own plan, born of her fury and frustration, to punish herself and disappear forever since she felt that she no longer deserved to live. "If there's anyone out there who can give me a reason to live, than come to me now, because I think I'm going to kill myself…"

The all-compassionate Buddha appeared by her side: "I have a mission for you, beautiful one. You can defeat any threat there is with your sword and that coat of diseases, since you know every malevolent trick in the book. You have no fear, so you will be a protective shield for every lost soul searching for compassion."

"You believe in me, after everything I did? You think I can bring protection to all the lost souls and the children, after I killed my own?" Palden Lhamo asked, weeping.

"Who better than you to protect those innocent creatures? Who knows a mother's pain better than you? Who knows all the tricks and secrets better than you?" the Buddha asked.

And with his blessing, Palden Lhamo was reborn, with her new name: "The Glorious Goddess."

That archetype of long, painful maternal suffering today protects everyone with her terrifying looks. She makes even fear itself afraid, so doubts and all negative things run away in horror at the very sight of her. That's why Western visitors find this alarming figure happily displayed all over Tibet … it's the same image the Dalai Lama took with him when he escaped from the Chinese occupation in 1959 …

IIIIIIIIIII

Jose closed the book and gazed at the candle illuminating the room, as its flame suddenly seemed to emanate a strange mysticism. He didn't know much about the Buddha or the Dalai Lama. He wasn't sure whether he should feel inspired by the story, or horrified. *Why did they need to include such grotesque details to propagate a myth? Why not use some other kinds of analogies*? he wondered, at the same time acknowledging his own ignorance with respect to other cultures and trying to understand something he was just learning about for the first time in his life.

He wondered, *Why would a man as important as the Dalai Lama want to take that story with him when he left China? What mysteries were hidden in that ancient culture*? Jose tried to identify the kind of rational logic his Western mind was accustomed to in the story, but he couldn't, so he blew out the candle and went to bed.

Maybe the next day he would be able to spend some more time with it and understand what he had read a bit better.

CHAPTER 5
A message for Sheleg

We have eyes but we don't see.
We have ears but we don't listen.
—King David

Although we often don't listen to our spirits, what if we did, and all that information was stored in our subconscious, waiting until we were ready to use it?

~ ~ ~

It was very early, and Jose opened his eyes feeling very differently than he had recently. When he woke up, he felt lonely and depressed, and he didn't understand why. It was very strange after so many peaceful and soothing days. He decided to take a shower and try to shake off the weird sensation that was gripping him.

He stayed in the shower for over an hour, spending most of the time with his eyes closed, trying to think positive thoughts that would return to him the inner peace that he seemed to have temporarily lost. But the harder he tried to dispel the negative feelings he was having, the more oppressive they seemed to become. "What's happening to me? There must be a way to take away these awful feelings ..."

IIIIIIIIIII

Sheleg was walking toward Central Park. It was early in the afternoon, and Jose had asked to meet him there; he had to tell him about all the strange things that were happening to him.

It was a sunny, breezy day. Joggers were out on the paths, while some people walked their dogs and others sat out on the grass just enjoying the day. It was a typical weekday in Central Park at the end of a long workweek.

Sheleg sat down on a bench to enjoy the scenery and watch the people walking by, each with their own special aura of energy. He had learned of this energy on a trip to India while in a remote village he wasn't even sure he could locate on a map, much less figure out how to get to again. He had walked for three days and three nights until he stumbled upon that village in the plains of Vindhyan, in central India.

There, he discovered a unique ethnic group who didn't have typical Hindu features and who spoke a very unusual dialect that was completely unknown to him. They were a very friendly people, and welcomed him. The village was like a spiritual oasis in the middle of the flatlands. The tribe seemed completely untouched by any kind of governmental or religious body. Clearly very few outsiders even knew this village existed, which was why Sheleg was extremely guarded about his experiences in that special place.

There, he met Mayir, a tall, dark-skinned young man who was always smiling. Like his fellow tribesmen, he usually walked around naked, although occasionally he would wear a loincloth. Sheleg was very surprised to see men and women walking around completely or mostly naked, in contrast to other parts of India. It was immediately evident to him that this particular tribe did not follow the same customs and traditions that were prevalent in the rest of the country.

Mayir's romantic partner, Astea, sewed a loincloth for Sheleg and presented it to him as a gift. Sheleg didn't hesitate in shedding his own clothes, since he didn't harbor any prejudices about nudity, either. He was learning a great deal from this culture; for example, it was there that he learned to eradicate the word "jealous" from his own relationship vocabulary, since that word only fomented one individual's false sense of possession over another, which obscured the couple's real feelings for each other. For Mayir and Astea's tribe, the pillars that sustained a relationship were love, freedom, understanding, and unity—principles that allowed them to fuse the energies of both people, in harmony and balance, to grow together as human beings. Thus this hidden village is also where Sheleg learned so much about soul mates. He learned that a couple's union, like procreation, was based on those principles and that marriage rites, spiritual leaders, or promises of eternal love were not needed in order to validate the quality of the relationship.

The most interesting thing to Sheleg was observing how each person in the village carried out their role without interfering with anyone else; everyone went about their business without any obstacles or complications. Everyone knew when to say yes or no, and everyone knew what to say and what to do at just the right time. The villagers were extraordinarily perceptive people who could just look at someone and be able to tell exactly what that person needed or wanted, and in his time there Sheleg discovered that they had learned how to do this by studying the energy of the auras. That was one of the great secrets that was passed down in their culture from one generation to the next.

The aura represented the individual; it was like a personal card, a projection of what was going on with that person at that moment. Within the village, everyone was an open book to everyone else, and that let their relationships develop very smoothly, without friction. It allowed them to spend more time exploring the eternal secrets of life, instead of wasting so much physical and mental energy on misunderstandings and confusion.

Mayir taught Sheleg how to concentrate so he could see auras, too. At first, it was a rather complex, mechanical process. But over time, it became something very simple and natural to him, just like blinking his eyes. It was easy to learn that skill there, since the people there had very strong auras, which could be easily seen. Sheleg understood this the day he left the tribe and came into contact with other people again. Some had auras that were so weak, they were practically imperceptible.

Sitting on the park bench, he remembered all of that, and he practiced reading the auras of other people in the park—

"Sheleg!" Jose yelled, spotting him and coming over.

"How are you, Jose?"

"I'm fine. Thanks for meeting me," he said breathlessly.

"No problem. You said on the phone that something really important was going on."

Getting right to the point, Jose began, "Yes. This morning I woke up feeling really low and confused. I spent almost the whole morning meditating, trying to understand what was happening to me. I took a long shower; I closed my eyes and let myself go. I was standing under the water for a really long time, trying to free myself of whatever it was I was feeling. I let my mind go blank for quite a while, until I began to feel my body relax, little by little. Everything around me began to fade away until I felt like I was floating, as if my body was made of foam."

Sheleg listened thoughtfully.

"A deep blue color was the background, and I sensed different smells. My soul was transported to a place completely unknown to me. There, I heard a clear voice that brought me much peace and tranquility. A few minutes later, I sensed your presence, too, and the voice clearly said that it had a message for me—that I should, in turn, pass along to you … I know what I'm about to say will sound irrational, because that's just what I thought, but this is exactly what happened," Jose said, pausing now to gather his thoughts.

He began again, "Like I said, I very clearly sensed the presence of a voice. That voice asked me to tell you that in a few days a child would be born who, as an adult, would cause many conflicts and confrontations. His only purpose would be to create chaos and confusion, and the only way to stop it from happening was to make sure the child was never born. And that's not all," Jose went on, "his non-existence would mean exactly the opposite—an extremely positive change in human evolution ..."

He trailed off and there was a brief pause while Sheleg looked intently at Jose, waiting for him to continue this very strange story.

"Then, I saw myself floating over a lake, and a white figure handed me a tablet with words inscribed on it. Then the voice told me that the person who had to do it was you."

Sheleg opened his eyes wide with surprise, since he thought the whole story was totally unreal and absurd. He said, "That story seems completely incongruous and senseless; it doesn't really mean anything to me. Are you sure it wasn't just a dream? Or you just imagined it?"

"That's what I thought, and then the wildest thing happened, separating fantasy from reality. The tablet had written on it the date, time, and names of the people and the hospital where all of this was going to happen—everything! It was all crystal clear. Then the figure moved away, and I started to become aware of my body again; I felt the water of the shower. I slowly opened my eyes, but I could still see the words that had been inscribed on the tablet in front of me. I got out of the shower and wrote down all that was written. I called that same hospital asked to speak with the person whose name I had written down, to confirm that it was true," Jose said. "They confirmed everything—all of it. I just told them the name I had in front of me, and they told me the rest. All the information I had already written down on that piece of paper ... it all matched up perfectly. That birth is already scheduled, and the names, date, and time were exactly as I had already written them down," he concluded emphatically.

Sheleg didn't say anything; he was puzzled and didn't know how this could be explained what it might mean. Jose broke the silence. "When I confirmed the information, I was totally stunned, in shock. I just couldn't believe it. We could even call again so you could see what I'm talking about ... I have my cell phone and the hospital's phone number; I thought it was really important that I do everything I could to make sure this wasn't all just my imagination running away with me."

Jose paused, and then added firmly, "I don't have the words to make you understand what I saw, but I can assure you that it was just as real as you and I sitting here right now."

Lost in his own thoughts, Sheleg pondered the circumstances that had brought him to New York. "Could your vision be related to what brought me here?" he asked, looking at Jose.

"I was wondering the same thing, and while I was walking over here, I remembered what you had said about us resolving something together. Maybe that challenge is just getting underway here. I don't know. I guess we'll have to wait and see what happens."

Jose's reasoning was sound. It added another perspective to the story. As bizarre and random as the message seemed, something told Sheleg that he couldn't ignore it, especially coming from his friend Jose, who had been the reason why he had come to New York in the first place. He knew he had to solve that enigma.

"Look, here's what we'll do. I'm going to go to the mountains for a few days. Don't tell anybody unless there's a real reason. Pay very close attention to anything you might see or hear, but stay relaxed and don't obsess. It's really important for me to understand what's going on here, and after spending some time in the city, I'd like to get away from it now—go somewhere quiet where I can reconnect with myself and try to figure out this puzzle," Sheleg said.

Jose nodded in agreement. "Okay, I understand. Here's all the information I wrote down; take it with you," he offered.

"Thanks." Sheleg took the folded piece of paper and put it in his bag.

"How long will you be gone?"

"I don't know; as long as it takes—but I doubt it will be any longer than two or three days. Definitely before the time and date listed here. Anyway, don't worry about me. I'll be back when I need to be back."

"Sure. Do you have any idea what all of this might mean?" Jose asked.

"No, I really don't. I'm trying to piece it together, but nothing fits."

"Alright. How can I get in touch with you if I need to?"

"Don't worry about it," Sheleg said with a mysterious smile.

Jose nodded. "Do you want me to drive you somewhere?" he offered.

He paused for a few seconds and replied. "That will be great, thanks."

IIIIIIIIIII

Sheleg set out for the Catskills at dusk, his head spinning, wondering what could possibly be going on. Nothing that Jose had told him had made any sense to him. Many questions ran through his mind, and he just grew more and more confused. The best thing Sheleg could do, he thought, would be to retreat to the mountains. He was sure he would unlock the key to solving the mystery in the peace and quiet of nature.

After walking for several hours he decided to sit down and rest on a little lookout point about halfway up the mountain, where he had a great view of the countryside spread out below. As he thought about his conversation with Jose, he remembered the letter he had written to his friend Marcia that he had started reading over but hadn't finished the day he had met the beggar at the café. He took the envelope with the copy of the letter out of his bag and continued reading, starting from where he had left off:

...But I'm getting ahead of myself, talking about the hospital. We had arrived at the location. It was absolutely silent. The driver shut off the jeep's lights, and the only source of illumination that night was the light from the other military vehicle, directly in front of us, trying to locate whoever might be hiding out there in the tall grass. I couldn't tell what was the most overwhelming in that moment: my fear, the total darkness, or the ominous silence that seemed to scream our arrival at the gates of hell. Nothing moved except the spotlight, which didn't seem to find anything. The place seemed to be suspended in eternity for the first time that night.

Suddenly I snapped out of the memories of my life story and back to harsh reality. The crackle of enemy gunfire compelled me to do what everyone else was doing: firing back into the darkness, hoping that a bullet might miraculously meet its target. Confusion and chaos translated into a blend of screams, explosions, uncertainty, and terror. I remember there was a mortar near me that when fired would light up the black sky like a burst of fireworks. I put the launcher on my shoulder and went to the back of the jeep. I turned and started to get out of the vehicle.

But when my right foot touched the ground, I felt the jeep starting to roll backward. I tried to move out of the way, but I couldn't. Something sharp and metallic hit me, and suddenly I couldn't breathe. I couldn't move, either, and all I could see was my knee folded into my chest and my weapon held fast against my bulletproof vest. The jeep that had been behind ours had collided with us, and I was trapped between both vehicles as they struggled to move in opposite directions.

While that was going on, I heard more gunfire and explosions, but that wasn't what I was worried about right then. I tried to shout to let someone know what was happening, but nothing came from my mouth. In the night's blackness, I could barely make out the back wheel of my jeep spinning without getting any traction, spewing out a cloud of dust, while the other jeep's engine roared in my ear, crushing me. No one had noticed what was happening to me; I was trapped and the pain was excruciating—so excruciating that I almost stopped feeling anything at all. I remember how I absurdly tried to push those jeeps off of me with my fingers. For the second time that night, eternity cast its shadow over that place.

Finally I noticed a soldier to my left. He was waving his hands frantically, trying to explain to the drivers what was going on, until finally my body was free and I collapsed to the ground.

What appeared to be the end of that agonizing, endless moment was actually just a brief pause. My foot had somehow gotten caught in the trailing jeep's grill, and as I fell to the ground, lying on my back, the jeep started dragging me. Fate was punishing me again, telling me I probably never should have gotten out of my vehicle.

After being dragged for several yards, I felt something tugging from behind me, and I was soon released from the latest nightmare. It was the same soldier as before, running behind me and grabbing onto my bulletproof vest. The soldier, a medic, pulled me down into a ditch by the side of the road and gave me first aid. I was finally safe, but I couldn't feel anything. It was as if my entire body was asleep.

I very clearly remember seeing nothing but black, even though my eyes were wide open. The view was not encouraging, but I felt a sense of peace that is very hard to describe … I was alive, and that was all that really mattered. Luckily, after a few minutes, my sight gradually started to come back. One of the drivers stayed with me and apologized for what had happened even as the battle still raged on. I told him he didn't have anything to apologize for, that it wasn't his fault. In circumstances like that, when life hangs by a thread, there are no guilty or innocent. He was crying; he didn't know what to say. He felt so guilty for what had happened, not understanding that he shouldn't have felt that way. Trying to take his mind off it, I asked if he would light me a cigarette, since he was already smoking one. He lit a cigarette and handed it to me. I tried to take a drag, but I couldn't. I guessed that I was worse off than I'd thought.

Hours later, I was lying in bed in a hospital. After an interminable medical exam, I finally drifted off to sleep. Some immeasurable amount of time passed …

I opened my eyes, without any sense of time and place, and saw Mia standing beside me. I smiled and closed my eyes again … I opened my eyes, I saw Charley, and closed them again … I opened my eyes a third time … and there was Ely … I sighed … and blinked … and I looked behind him … and there I saw Jose. He didn't say a word; he was hiding behind someone. He didn't want me to see the pain he was in, and only then did I understand how serious the situation was. They had traveled from the capital, where they had gotten the news of what had happened. They had been urged to come to the hospital as quickly as possible, with no guarantee that they'd ever see me alive again.

Two parallel worlds were coming together in that moment: my world, which consisted of opening my eyes once in a while to catch a glimpse of the stars of the movie called "The Story of My Life;" and theirs, the stars of the movie, praying for me to get out of this alive. There they all were, day and night, hour after hour, never leaving me for a single minute, aware of a reality of which I knew nothing.

On the third day, the internal bleeding that hadn't wanted to slow down, that had been threatening my life, finally heeded the prayers of everyone present and decided to stop. The first battle was over, but the second was just beginning. I spent six months in the hospital, lying in bed and unable to move. I had countless surgeries and endured indescribable pain. But it was all worth it, since over that very long time, the ones I remembered so much on that twenty-second of June, 1988, who the wind whispered I would never see again, were by my side, and they didn't leave me alone for a single minute throughout the whole recovery period.

I could never forget any of them, and especially the ones who are no longer here—Mia, Charley, and Ely—because if it hadn't been for them, I wouldn't be here either. Only they know how much I miss them …

Forever yours,

Sheleg

CHAPTER 6

In the mountains

"You can believe in stones,
as long as you don't throw them at others"

You can't change others' lives,
but others' lives can change when they see inside of you.
Whoever sees your light will want to find the light within themselves, too,
because everyone should shine with their own light.

~ ~ ~

Sheleg had been in the mountains for two days in a very peaceful, solitary spot. A river, which would eventually arrive at Kaaterskill Falls, flowed by the western side of the mountain, and rock formations were all around. Colorful birds that flew through the spring air and trees of many different shapes and sizes, which were surrounded by blankets of wildflowers on the ground, breathed life into the beautiful place. Small forest animals and playful squirrels gazed at him, curious, and occasionally approached him cautiously. The trek to this secluded place had been long and dangerous because of the sharp outcroppings of rock, loose stones, and because it was a place where the slightest error could have very serious consequences. He had set up camp in a small clearing surrounded by hazelnut trees and some other trees that bore small, red fruit that he could eat. The few supplies he had brought with him were sufficient. He bathed in the river, renewing his energies by washing off the negative ones. He passed the time taking hikes on the mountain, sitting on the ground, laying back against any tree, or simply looking up at the sky, not thinking of anything.

When night began to fall, Sheleg lit a small fire with wood he had foraged from the forest floor. It was chilly, and aside from being a source of warmth, the fire lit up the night with a spectacular array of shapes, sounds, and colors. The night was dark, and he could perfectly make out the reds and yellows as they arose from the burning sticks. The wind gently blew, blending the cold air with the vibrant colors and scents, creating a new, amazing gamut of sensations that Sheleg enjoyed immensely. In the sky overhead, the stars seemed to twinkle with the fire's rhythm, while lights shot across the sky, carrying with them the wishes of those who gazed upon them from the faraway city.

Sheleg closed his eyes and took some deep breaths before beginning the meditation he had been planning. He was setting out on a journey across the universe. Years of studying and experience had taught him how to disconnect from his body and connect with other dimensions. He breathed deeply, his inhalations gradually slowing down. The air he drew into his lungs grew thinner and thinner, and his temperature gradually rose with each exhalation. The sounds and smells of the forest night grew less intense, a sign that soon he would not perceive them at all.

Gradually, he was disconnecting each internal filament of his being that connected with physical sensation. He was mentally scanning each part of his body, sending them the message that they should block out all feeling—no cold, no heat, no drowsiness. No exertion, no good, no bad—no nothing. Only a fine thread of energy would remain active, allowing the lifeline between the body and soul to remain active. That link, a fine, yellow thread, is what we call conscience—that part of us for which anything is possible. Soon Sheleg no longer felt the mountain air's cold or the fire's warmth, and he could no longer hear the sounds of the night. He had freed himself from all sensations, his body had grown lighter, and his spirit had separated from his body, rising higher and higher.

Sheleg could clearly see the lights of the faraway city while the process progressively accelerated, until finally he reached a place where he transcended time and space, connecting with another dimension. He saw lights, many lights all around, while behind him was the ephemeral, glowing tunnel he had traveled, now transformed into a tiny point, where Sheleg knew the now-microscopic planet earth could be found.

He had experienced this state several times before, and he was repeating it now in his quest for answers. This time his destination was a very distant place of incomparable beauty, with purple sand dunes and strange craters of many shapes and incredible colors. Various trees that were similar to pines dotted the dreamy landscape. They were green and triangular, although their green was very different from the shades of green he knew on earth. The trees gave off an exquisite fragrance that was impossible to describe, just like everything he saw in that amazing place defied description.

He was getting closer, about to arrive at the place where he hoped to find an explanation for his friend Jose's bizarre vision. From far away he began to make out the purples. They looked like undulating waves in a giant lake, illuminated sporadically by cylindrical beams of light, flashing intermittently, that seemed to have no source. He gradually came closer and closer, enjoying looking at the different landscapes as they unfolded before him—every tree, every color, until finally he reached the surface and fused completely with it.

He felt like a little boy. He was very calm and content in that fine sand. It wasn't rough at all, and it didn't cling to the skin; you could completely immerse yourself in it and then shake it all off. The trees were very tall and lush. Halos of bright, white light formed at the very tops of them, slowly rotating around the trees and changing color as they dropped toward the ground, finally disappearing around the lowest branches and leaving a beautiful trace of glowing brown. As these descended, other halos formed again at the top of the tree and began their descent; the cycle continued uninterrupted in all the trees.

Like the sand, the trees did not have a solid structure. You could literally enter the trees through hexagon-shaped cavities that ran along the whole length of the trunks. Inside, a yellow chamber in the middle of the tree could transport you to different dimensions, since they were all interconnected. The scent inside the trees was very different from the scent that emanated from their exteriors; is was subtler, and soothing. Each different scent represented a portal to another dimension, and each dimension was represented by its own color. Sheleg had learned that there were ten different dimensions in total and that the presence of what we know as God lay beyond the tenth dimension.

The first dimension, found on the lowest part of the tree, was brown in color. That was where the physical universe was found—where time, space, the planets, stars, and galaxies existed. Humans live in that dimension, and that is where we begin to evolve.

Sheleg stayed in the tree's yellow interior and remembered the first time he had ever been to that incredible place …

It was almost twelve years ago. Sitting beside the Dead Sea, which divides Israel from Jordan, watching the sun slowly dip below the horizon, Sheleg suddenly felt someone tap his shoulder. Turning around, he saw an old man with a long beard dressed in clothing typical of the people who live in the desert.

"What are you doing in such a lonely place, my boy?" the old man asked.

Surprised by the visitor, he answered, "Over there," he pointed, "there are lots of people. Tourists, visitors, work sites, machines … I just wanted to get away and find some silence. I walked for a long time, and when I noticed it was almost nightfall, I decided to sit down and rest to watch the sunset. And how did you get here, sir?" he asked back, squinting against the setting sun.

Ignoring the question, the mysterious man inquired, "Do you want to go somewhere really interesting?"

"Of course, I'd love to!" Sheleg exclaimed, nodding as he rose to his feet.

"I can take you there, but it's a long, rocky road, and it will be dark soon. Do you think you're prepared?"

The warning gave Sheleg pause, and he remembered that he hadn't eaten anything in hours. Then he noticed he was thirsty, and suddenly he felt confused and didn't know what to do. "Do you have any water, sir?" he asked, trying to buy a little time while he decided whether he should return to his hostel or follow this old man, who had an air of wisdom about him.

"Water is no problem; there will be plenty along the way," the man said cryptically.

Something inside of Sheleg compelled him to follow this man. He didn't know what it was, but he felt reassured in his presence. So without giving it another thought, Sheleg decided to accept his invitation.

They walked for several hours into the night. The old man was barefoot. The path, obscured by the dark, silent night, was dry and rocky, just as the old man had warned. Sheleg was very tired, in contrast to his guide, who showed no signs of fatigue at all. Sheleg couldn't figure out where he got so much energy.

"What is your name, sir?" Sheleg asked.

"You can call me Ari-cadu."

"Do you live around here?"

"Yes."

"Do you have a family?" Sheleg asked, but this time he got no response. After a moment he added, "I guess you don't like to talk much."

"I do, but talking now would be a distraction, depriving you of the beauty of the path. We'll have plenty of time to talk later," Ari-cadu replied.

"I understand, but to tell you the truth, it's so dark that I can't really see the beauty you're talking about …"

"Look up."

Sheleg raised his gaze and saw millions of stars in the sky. He had never before seen a sky so filled with them, each one vibrating at its own frequency, and from where he stood there wasn't one inch of space from one to the next. It was unspeakably beautiful. "Yes, it's incredible! I hadn't noticed; I was so busy trying to see the path that I didn't realize."

"Start to remember these lessons, son. Often, the dark, rocky roads of life keep us from seeing the real beauty that's all around us," the desert man explained.

"Yes, but if we don't look at the path, we could fall down …"

"That's true, and that's why you need to learn how to see the path and the stars that watch over it at the same time. If you focus on just one point, you can't be objective, and you'll lose the ability to have balance in your life."

"Yes, I understand, that seems true," Sheleg said hesitantly.

They kept on walking, while Sheleg tried to see what the old man called "the beauty of the night." He felt like an explorer, first looking up, then down, then to the left and right. He tried to convince himself that the beauty of the night existed, but just then what he wanted more than anything was to get something to eat and to lie down and fall asleep, since he was very hungry and exhausted.

But finally they reached their destination.

"This is the place I was telling you about," the desert man said.

"But it's so dark; I can't see anything. Do you have a lantern or flashlight?" Sheleg asked, surprised and frustrated.

"You don't need one. Follow me."

They walked along a dark path and went into a cave. It was so dark Sheleg couldn't even see his hand as he passed it right in front of his face. He commented, "Sir, this is really too dark. Outside, I could see the path a little bit with the stars and moonlight, but I can't even see to the tip of my nose in here."

"Don't worry, there's nothing around you that you might bump into," Ari-cadu soothed. "You can walk without fear."

"Are you sure?"

"As sure as the perfectly smooth floor beneath your feet."

Sheleg was stunned by the sudden realization. "That's true! I hadn't noticed, but it is completely smooth. I can't feel even a single grain of sand."

"Before, you couldn't stop looking at and feeling your way along the path for one second, and now you ignore it completely, trying so hard to see what's in front of you," Ari-cadu said with a laugh.

"I think I'm not going to score any points with you tonight, sir!"

The old man laughed at this. They walked for a few more minutes, until they arrived at a vast, brightly lit cavern. Sheleg blinked, accustoming himself to the light, and the exclaimed, "My God! What is this? It's incredible! Where are we?"

There weren't any candles, or fires, or electric lights, or windows. The strange, brilliant light emanating from the smooth, natural rock walls was all that illuminated this mysterious place.

The sage explained, "Here beats the heart of the planet. All of the stories of humanity have been written and continue to be written here: its past, present, and future. Those of us who have inhabited this cave have received messages, and we have written them down on countless scrolls."

"And you are one of them?" Sheleg asked, surprised.

"I am one of many, and what I am doing will be revealed over the course of many years, just like what has been written in the past is still in the process of being revealed today."

"But why wait? Why not reveal everything right now, all at once? There are so many people that might really need these lessons now! The information you have out here could mean a radical change for many people, no?"

"No, my son, the time is not right … we are not ready yet. We still have much to learn, and this place and all that is written here would be lost if we don't wait for the right moment to act."

"I think I understand," Sheleg said, contemplating. Then he asked, "So why did you bring me here?"

The old man smiled at him. This young novice had taken quite a while to ask the most important question of the night, and this was just what Ari-cadu had been waiting for. The question carried a great deal of significance. "So that you can deliver part of the message," Ari-cadu replied.

Sheleg looked at him, stunned, and asked, "But you said that it was secret."

The old man leaned forward and said very deliberately, "The existence of this place is a secret, and so are the scribes, but the essence and meaning of the messages are not. They belong to everyone who is ready to listen. You will carry them in your heart, and you will learn to pass them on. From this moment, that will be your task," Ari-cadu explained.

"I understand … but how do you know you can trust me? And, why me? I mean, it's not that I don't want to … it's just that …" his voice trailed off while the older man smiled in the face of Sheleg's very understandable confusion.

"Because it is written that one day, a day like today, a young man in search of truth will sit to watch the sunset on the Rock of Light."

"On the Rock of Light?" Sheleg asked, and then he remembered. "Ah, of course!"

The old man clarified, "Yes, that rock you were sitting on when I came up to you is known as the Rock of Light."

"And it was written in the scrolls that I would be there?"

"Not only that. The life story of each and every one of us can be found within the scrolls, down to the smallest detail. That is why they are so important—because they contain all of the secrets of human race."

More and more questions popped into Sheleg's mind. "And how do you receive the information?"

"This place is like a powerful magnet of energy. It absorbs the energy of creation and allows you to hear the voice of the universe."

"That's incredible. This all seems like a dream … and where do the scrolls come from? And the ink, clothing, food …?" he asked, looking around him with wonder. "This place is so remote, and you don't seem like the type who runs off to the market every day to shop," Sheleg said with a smile.

The older man smiled in return and explained, "Many secrets are held within these caves, and I understand why you're so curious. But for now, your mission is to continue your travels throughout the world, carrying the message to everyone who wants to listen."

"What's the message I'm supposed to deliver? How do I do it?" Sheleg asked.

"First, you have to understand that you can't change others' lives, but others' lives can change when they see inside of you. Whoever sees your light will want to find the light within themselves, too, because everyone should shine with their own light. Help all those who have the genuine desire to find it."

"So, what exactly should I tell them?" he asked, his voice barely a whisper.

"You know as well as I do; I don't have to explain that to you. You were brought to this place because deep inside you already knew it was here. Now you carry its strength, its energy, and above all, its truth. So every time you need it, get in touch with your heart. That has the same form as this cave, and you will find this place there, as well," Ari-cadu explained as he walked away. As he finished speaking, he disappeared down a long side tunnel.

A few minutes later, the scribe reappeared, carrying some scrolls. "This is one of the scriptures," he said, handing it to Sheleg.

"Can I touch them?" the novice asked, surprised.

"Of course you can, my son." The older man smiled at his innocence.

"I'm just asking because I don't want to damage them, and I would imagine these are sacred and should be treated as such, right?"

"Of course they're sacred, my son. As sacred as the bee buzzing over a flower, or the earth where the flowers spring from. They are as sacred as a newborn baby, or the cane that an old man leans on … as sacred as a pebble in your shoe, or the moon shining in the sky."

"I understand, sir. Everything is sacred. We tend to venerate books and temples, but we can't maintain the same attitude about everything around us, right?" Sheleg observed.

"That's right. We are very careful about how we behave in places we consider sacred, and we forget that wherever we are on the entire planet is a sacred place and deserves the same respect."

"I've never seen it that way, but it's true," Sheleg nodded, looking at the scrolls and unrolling one of them. "It's beautiful! I've never seen anything like this … although," he said, studying it, "I've got to admit I can't understand what's written here."

"I know. It's written in Aramaic, and in other places in medieval Hebrew. But don't worry; your soul understands perfectly well. What you're looking at are codes, not just letters and words. Connect with them through your spirit and you'll understand what I mean," Aricadu explained.

"You can't read it either?" Sheleg asked tentatively.

"Everyone receives what is written there the way he is supposed to receive it. Some people can understand every letter, every single word, each line, while others can connect with the meaning through visualization," the old man explained. Then there was quiet for a few moments as he waited for Sheleg's next question.

"Does this have something to do with The Book of Splendor?"

"Yes, part of these scriptures have been included in that holy book, and that's why some people consider it one of the most important books in all of history."

"What do you think of it?" Sheleg asked.

"What I think of it is totally irrelevant. What's important is how the people who read it and want to understand it feel about it."

"Does that book belong to anyone in particular?"

"We all belong to it, and it's teachings are available to everyone who wants to learn them," Ari-cadu explained.

There was a short silence. Sheleg felt as if the more questions he asked, the less he understood, and the less he understood, the more questions he had, so he decided to keep on trying to figure it out.

"What does God mean to you?" Sheleg asked the wise old man.

"God is something beyond our rational comprehension, and everything that exists is nothing more than a manifestation of God's existence."

"I understand." Then, getting back to the matter physically at hand, Sheleg asked, "Can you teach me how to use the scrolls?"

"You're holding them in your hands. Let them guide you; the scrolls know how to show you the way," the scribe instructed.

The scrolls were the color of golden honey, and perfectly formed letters were written in black ink on them. Sheleg reexamined the scroll he held, now studying it more closely than before. This time he noticed how the sharp contrast between the writing and the scroll's surface seemed to pulsate. As he held the scroll close up, and then farther away, he saw how the letters seemed to roll from one side to the other, forming waves. He felt like something was gently massaging his brain, pleasantly stimulating his senses and relaxing him. He looked up and closed his eyes. Now he felt that the entire cave seemed to be pulsating in time with the letters, rhythmically expanding and contracting. He breathed deeply, looked at the old man, and closed his eyes again, resting his hand on top of the scroll. Within just a few minutes, he found himself in the yellow chamber within the tree trunk on the purple planet. He was sitting in the Tree of Life …

IIIIIIIIIII

Thus was Sheleg's first visit to this planet, and the memory of the encounter always flooded his mind every time he set foot there again.

Now he glimpsed a dimension the color of blue to his right, and he entered into it. The attribute this dimension represented was the desire to give; everything you asked for there was granted, without limit. When he left that dimension, he went to the other side of the yellow chamber, into the dimension on the left. This one was the color of red, and it represented limitation and judgment—the exact opposite of the blue dimension. Sheleg understood that beauty, harmony, and balance could be found in the tree's center, that place known as Zeir-Anpin, where six of the ten dimensions meet.

Sheleg now tried to reach the three higher dimensions, but a magnetic energy force pushed him back to the middle zone. Discovering his path blocked, he decided to go back to the lowest-level dimension, the brown one outside the tree where the planet was. He understood that he wasn't ready to ascend to the higher dimensions and that even though the spirit is free and the universe is available to anyone who wants to know it, everything has to happen in its own time.

IIIIIIIIIII

During his first ever long journey through space from the earth to this alien planet that housed the link to other dimensions, Sheleg had discovered that the earth's solar system had a protective shield around it that kept the destructive effects of man from breaking through. No matter how many bombs humans set off, how many viruses they created, how much hate they projected, or how many missiles they launched, everything that was not in balance and harmony with the universe would remain encased within that cosmic sphere of energy that housed the solar system and all its components. Sheleg recalled from the scrolls that this phenomenon existed in other parts of the universe, as well. Further, there was no action or force that he knew of that could circumvent these shields or break through the barriers of energy around any of the planets.

Sheleg climbed out of the tree, leaving the yellow dimension. He picked up a handful of purple sand, and as he slowly let it fall from his fingers he wondered why, over the course of all of his journeys across the universe, he had never come across a single outer space being. Even though he was convinced that they existed, he had never seen one. Maybe, he reasoned, the shields made any alien invasion of the earth from outer space, or vice-versa, impossible. Maybe the barriers kept all the intelligent life-forms apart from each other completely. In any case, he still had faith that one day he would get his chance to meet a being not from earth.

He also reflected on man's landing on the moon. He thought about how that small step for man had been a giant leap for mankind. And although there was no need to minimize that accomplishment, it had to be acknowledged that the human race had not lived up to many responsibilities in its own home, while dedicating enormous efforts and resources outside of it. *If all the toil and creative energy we put into technology, political campaigns, wars, fashion, and gossip were instead applied to personal growth and understanding, our lives would be much simpler and much more satisfying,* Sheleg thought to himself.

His thoughts turned to the reason for his visit to this distant planet. His imaginary friend, Allyson, came to mind. She could probably help him to find the answer he so desperately sought. She had popped into Sheleg's life one day when he was on the purple planet and he had wanted to share the experience with someone. *Who better than an imaginary friend to share with when you want to be alone? They understand you perfectly, and are always in tune with your thoughts,* Sheleg mused.

"Hey, Allyson, where are you?" Sheleg murmured.

"I'm here, behind you. It's so good to see you!" a sweet voice replied.

"I'm here to try and get a question answered," he told her.

"What do you need to know?"

He told her the whole story that Jose had told him. "It's confusing, and I really don't know what it's all about," Sheleg said after concluding the anecdotal story.

"Try this," Allyson suggested. "Draw two circles in the sand. One will represent the 'Yes' and the other the 'No.' Ask the question you would like answered, and wait and see what happens."

Sheleg was quiet for a few minutes, and then responded, "Yes, that's not a bad idea; it could be a good place to start."

He traced two large circles in the sand. He wrote "Yes" in the circle on the right and "No" in the one on the left. He sighed deeply, closed his eyes, lowered his head, and offered his question to the universe. Instantly, everything around him went black.

CHAPTER 7

Back to the city

"Before God created the universe,
first existed His desire to do so."

The smallest material expression
is not the atom, nor the electron, nor the quark;
it is thought, and desire:
that infinitesimal point where everything begins.

~ ~ ~

Dawn was breaking. His eyes still closed, Sheleg could heard the birds singing and the river flowing. The night had passed in a fraction of an instant. He slowly opened his eyes when he heard some strange sounds a few yards away. He raised himself up, leaning on his elbows. He was startled to see a lynx and a wolf staring at him intently. Sheleg blinked, trying to clear his blurry vision. He didn't understand what was happening. He took a few deep breaths, rubbed his eyes, and looked up again.

The two animals were still there, just looking at him silently without moving. Sheleg sat up, and to his even greater surprise, he saw three circles made out of sticks lying on the ground near him.

Two of them were similar to what he had traced in the purple sand, but here there was a third, located right in between the other two. The animals were sitting in that circle. The lynx picked up a stick in his mouth and put it in front of Sheleg, while the wolf let out a long howl. Then they got up and trotted off into the forest. Sheleg gazed at the circle where the animals had just been sitting and shook his head slowly, sighing. He looked up at the sky and somewhat ironically thanked the universe for the confounding response. His interpretation of all of this was very simple: he had to decide for himself what he should do; the decision rested in his hands.

After trying to make sense out of what had happened, Sheleg gathered up his things, putting the small stick the lynx had offered to him in his bag, and began his long descent. He had several hours to think about what he should do. The long walk might offer him some much-needed clarity.

Time was growing short, and for the first time in a long time he felt like it was chasing at his heels. He stopped and tried to get his thoughts in order, since everything had its moment, and he had to calm down. Confusion and frenzy were not good counselors, and he had to make sure he didn't lose perspective on the situation. He had to go with the flow, not letting uncertainty prompt him to start down the wrong path. He reestablished his own unhurried rhythm and continued on his journey.

After a long time walking, near the end of his descent, Sheleg spotted four teenage boys approaching him. They looked like they were up to no good. They carried baseball bats, and two of them even had knives prominently displayed on their belts. Sheleg stayed calm.

"What's in the bag?" one of them asked, challenging him.

"Nothing that's worth anything," Sheleg replied.

"Oh, you think you're funny," another one of them said.

"Is there something I can help you with?" Sheleg asked.

"Of course!" a third boy exclaimed. "Give us everything you have and stop asking questions. If you don't like it, it will be my pleasure to drag you by your hair and mop you into the river."

Sheleg shrugged. "Is this all you want? Take it. If it'll make you happy, you can have it. You can put your bats and knives down; that won't be necessary."

His assailants looked at each other, wondering if this man even understood how much danger he was in. He was certainly in no position to be telling them what to do.

"Here, take it," Sheleg offered. "One, two, three, four … let's see, I think I have some coins in here, too. You can have it all—the bag, the clothes, the blanket. I don't know how useful this will be to you, but this is really all I have. The one thing I'm not going to give you is this stick that some animals gave me up on the mountain this morning when I woke up," he explained. The four boys didn't know whether to laugh or to beat him up. "This stick is part of a very important message, and I think I should save it until I clear something up," he said, laughing in his mind.

Now all four boys looked confused. Sheleg thought they must think of him as some poor lunatic who didn't even know where he was. Suddenly they decided to go back the way they had come, turning and leaving without even taking the few dollars that had been offered, much less the bag with his junk in it.

Sheleg watched as they walked away. He called after them, "Anyway, I'm going to see my friend Jose later on today; I'm sure he could give you a lot more money than I could."

The boy who hadn't yet spoken turned around, shaking his head in disgust. He called back, "I thought all the drugs and booze was making *me* crazy. Ha!"

Sheleg kept walking, analyzing the incident. He wondered how many people had been attacked or hurt by those guys. Those teens were nothing more than a reflection of a society in a state of moral decay, manifested as misery, vandalism, drug addiction, and alcohol abuse. Sheleg thought that the decline of human, social, and family values based on love, education, and understanding was the main cause of that regrettable reality. All over the planet, this profound lack translated into wars, disease, and violence in some places, or corruption, fanaticism, and repression in others.

Sheleg thought, *Could this incident be a sign, pointing out the right thing to do*? Suddenly, the word "coincidence" popped into his head, big and loud, like a brightly-lit billboard.

"Coincidences ..." he murmured. Something was telling him that he had to be more aware of these, of every sign and synchronicity, since he knew very well how important they were. They could help shed light on the answer to his puzzling enigma.

In the cave, the wise man Ari-cadu had explained to him their importance ...

IIIIIIIIIII

"Coincidences are signs that we leave along the way in our life's journey, helping us find the right road."

"What do we leave?" Sheleg asked, confused. "You mean, they are signs that we find, right?"

"I understand your confusion," he said, smiling gently. "In the transition from your past life into this one, you left these signs yourself so that they could show you the right path."

"I don't understand, sir," Sheleg said with a shrug.

"There is a period of transition between your past life and the present one. That is when your soul ceases inhabiting your body and transcends into a perfect dimension where there is no time or space, and where the past, present, and future coexist. It is precisely in this dimension where we can clearly see the 'why' of all things, and our own virtues and weaknesses. In this way, we can plan and rewrite what the right path is, which we should follow in order to reach our objective on the earthly plane. That is, ultimately, the evolution of the soul."

"You mean that every one of us writes his own destiny?" Sheleg asked.

"You will learn over time that yes, we do. But for now, you can think of it not so much as writing our own destiny, but as writing the directions for the perfect journey that we were meant to travel," the old man explained. "Coincidences are signs we put there ourselves, and they guide us back to the right road each time we lose our way."

"Do you mean that even though there is a perfect road for us, we could also travel down another road?"

"Yes, and this is what we know as free will—the power to choose in this life, on this earthly plane, the path we want to follow. But you must understand something very important: the more we stray from our own perfect road, the more chaotic and confusing our lives become. And the more closely we follow that road, the opposite happens—your life's journey starts to flow along peacefully and happily, in perfect harmony."

"Of course! Now I get it! Chaos and happiness are also signs, right?" Sheleg exclaimed. "They tell us whether or not we're on the right path … or am I wrong?"

"No, you're not wrong; they are very basic signs that life gives us so we can get on the right road."

The walls of the cave kept on pulsating with that peculiar light emanating from the rocks as Sheleg delved deeper into the matter.

"I have another question, sir … I'm sorry for asking so many," he said, wide-eyed, as Ari-cadu chuckled at his apology. "If such a perfect dimension exists where the soul goes after it leaves the body, then why do we come back to this hard, tumultuous world instead of just staying there forever?"

The wise old man paused. His gaze seemed to search around that dazzling place for just the right words. Finally he replied, "In order to develop and tone a muscle, it's not enough to know the exercise routines that we must do; we have to actually practice them to get results. It's the same thing with the soul. Even though it may see things very clearly in the other dimension, that does not imply its tacit evolution. For this, there needs to be action. That is why the soul inhabits a physical body. In this plane, which functions as a training ground, the limits of the senses, time and space, and the material world offer resistance, compelling the soul to grow as it searches for its true reason for being and tries to meet its objective."

"Is that evolution really so important?"

"Of course, since one day, that evolution will bring your soul—your energy—to a place where the greatest satisfaction you have ever experienced in this physical plane will be absolutely nothing compared with the infinite satisfaction you will feel there. But to get there, you have to be prepared. Humanity has to be prepared; we all have to be …"

That's how Sheleg remembered his conversation with the wise man, Ari-cadu. But now his mind came back to earth, and he wondered again how he would get back to the city in time for the momentous event he was supposed to be a part of. The universe will provide a way, Sheleg thought. What is meant to happen, will happen.

A few moments later, a car passed him on the road, slowing down and stopping a short distance ahead. As Sheleg approached, he saw that the license plate read "MCE 333." When he got to the car, the driver, a kindly looking middle-aged woman, rolled down the window and said, "Howdy, stranger. Do you need a ride somewhere? I'm going into the city, and I can take you, if you like."

Sheleg smiled, amazed at the coincidence. Coincidences are signs, helping us find the right road, Sheleg remembered. He said to the woman, "Yes, that's great. Thank you very much," and got in the car.

The ride back was uneventful, and Sheleg found himself in New York City just after nightfall. He thanked the woman again as he climbed out of the car. "Is there anything I can do for you in return?" he asked.

She shook her head. "Oh, it's nothing. I remember a time once when I needed help on the road from a stranger. I'm just paying it back."She drove off, and Sheleg was left alone. Now that he was in town, he felt that he had to call Jose …

He was about to go into a small restaurant when he heard somebody behind him shout, “Hey, Sheleg! How’re you doing?”

Although the voice sounded familiar, he couldn’t immediately identify it. He turned around, and there was Gabriel, the young man Jose had almost collided with that first day in the city in Jose’s office.

“When the moon is full, lighting up the sky, we’ll meet again,” Gabriel reminded him, smiling and gesturing toward the sky, where a perfectly circular, brilliant moon beamed, confirming his words.

“I remember that,” Sheleg said, giving him a hug. “It’s nice to run into you like this!”

“I’m happy to see you, too.”

“What are you doing here?” Sheleg asked. “Do you live in the neighborhood?”

“Yes, I just live on the next block. I came down to pick up a few things at the deli, and while I was there I bought a lottery ticket,” he said, showing it to Sheleg.

“What do you think you’ll do with the money if you win?” Sheleg asked.

“Well, I know I couldn’t exactly change the world with the prize money, but I think it would be enough to make a few people around me very happy,” Gabriel said.

Sheleg now posed a challenge: “And if the future of the whole planet was in your hands through this money, then would you change the world?”

“The future of the planet in my hands?” Gabriel repeated. “I think you should know the answer to that better than me, my friend.”

Sheleg raised his eyebrows. “What do you mean?”

“I mean, the future of the planet cannot be in the hands of just one person; each individual is master of his own destiny and his own circumstances,” Gabriel said emphatically.

“Yes! Of course! You’re right!” Sheleg exclaimed, something clicking in his mind. "How come that hadn't occurred to me before? How could I not have noticed something so obvious?"

"That tends to happen, especially when there is doubt and confusion," Gabriel said sagely. "Then even the most obvious things can be obscured in that fog."

"You are so right; it's so true."

"Yes, but where are you going with all of this?" Gabriel asked.

"It's a long story, but you just cleared something up for me that I've been searching really hard for …"

"If that's the case, then I'm glad." Gabriel nodded and smiled, and then asked, "Do you want to get a cup of coffee and tell me more about it?"

Just then, an ambulance raced down the street, its sirens blaring. A very strange feeling came over Sheleg. He turned to look at the ambulance, and he saw that it had a number on its side: 30303. Then he noticed a taxi parked next to the curb, with the number 3339. In that instant, he overheard a passerby say, "That's the third time I've seen that ambulance drive by in less than an hour."

Enveloped in that strange feeling, Sheleg looked at Gabriel, thinking about the sequence of these coincidences, and said, "I'm sorry, but I've got to go; there's something very important I've got to finish. There's no time, but I'll explain everything later."

His friend nodded. "Don't worry, go and do what you have to do."

Sheleg rushed away and climbed into the taxi parked near the curb. "Can you follow that ambulance, please?" he asked the driver.

"Sure!" the driver, an older man with a cheerful expression, said amiably.

Sheleg looked out the window to wave good-bye to Gabriel, but he wasn't there anymore. He tried to spot him, but he didn't see him anywhere. Surprised, he slowly shook his head, not understanding how that very intriguing person could have disappeared so fast.

CHAPTER 8

At the hospital

"Love is a way of life."

Love is a pure emotion and an attitude toward life. Don't allow impurities like egoism, resentment, envy, prejudices, hatred, or lies to alter the purity of this feeling, which allows you to be in perfect balance and harmony with the universe.

~ ~ ~

The taxi weaved through Manhattan's busy streets.

"Are you of Portuguese descent?" Sheleg asked, reading the driver's name on the identification card displayed on the Plexiglas window.

"Yes, but I grew up in Venezuela, in a town on the beach called Cuyagua. I came to New York thirty-three years ago."

Sheleg smiled. It was the fourth time his fated numbers had come up in less than a minute. The signs were pointing the way.

"My name is Antonio Figueira, but everybody calls me Tony ever since I came to New York, so people think I must be Italian. Ha ha, that's how things are here!" the cabbie explained. He went on, "My parents were born citizens of Portugal, in the Azor Islands. It's a beautiful place. Not very well-known, but really pretty."

Sheleg was distracted, still thinking quietly about his encounter with Gabriel, repeating his friend's words over and over in his head.

Why didn't I think of that before? he thought to himself. *Every human being's destiny is in his own hands, not in mine, or anyone else's …*

Then he wondered, *How many lives could have been spared if not for this misinterpretation of life? How many wars would not have been waged in God's name? How many religious fanatics would not have blown up their bodies to glorify their God's will*?

The taxi kept following behind the ambulance at a short distance, doing its best to keep up. Sheleg was pensive, now with a new thought on his mind: *So what could everything that Jose told me mean? What's behind all of that*? There were still so many questions that needed answers, and Sheleg hoped that at this journey's final destination the answer to the enigma could be found.

The taxi pulled up in front of the hospital's emergency room. The ambulance was parked just in front of them. Two paramedics opened the rear door to the ambulance and took out a gurney. A woman was lying on it. Then a tall, good-looking man climbed out, clutching a shoulder bag, trying to soothe the woman. "It's alright, darling. We're here. Everything's going to be fine."

"*Nothing's … going to be … fine*!" she wailed between synchronized breaths.

Sheleg got out of the taxi, leaving the door ajar. He told the driver, "I'll be right back."

Tony stepped out of the car and leaned on the door, a bit disconcerted. A few customers had jumped out on him without paying before, and he didn't want it to happen again.

Just then, a man wearing a straw hat came up to him and asked, "Excuse me, are you available?"

"That guy that just got out still has to pay me; I'm waiting for him to come back."

"Don't worry about it. I'll pay for him," the man replied without any hesitation.

"But it's almost twenty dollars!" Tony said.

"It's no problem. Let's go; he probably doesn't even remember you're out here," he said with a grin.

"Okay!" They both got into the taxi and the man handed Tony the money. "Thanks a lot," Tony said as he drove away from the hospital.

The cab was reflected in the rounded, glass-walled building across the street as it disappeared into the city streets.

IIIIIIIIIII

Sheleg approached the couple as they wheeled the pregnant woman through the entryway and quietly said to the tall man, "Please let me help you with this."

Without giving it a thought, the man let the bag slip from his shoulder and handed it to Sheleg. The woman kept screaming.

"Ahhh! This is killing me! Why in the world did I ever want to be a mother?"

The paramedics exchanged knowing glances and tried to suppress smiles. This scene was repeated over and over with nearly every woman they brought to the hospital who was about to give birth. The tall man was relieved to see them smiling. For him, this was a totally new experience. He was a first-time father, and seeing them grinning set his mind at ease. He now understood that his wife's cries of pain—sounds he had never heard from her before—were just part of the process.

They rolled the gurney down the hospital's hallways, and along the way the nurses were busy preparing the patient, exchanging information, and talking on the radio. Everything seemed to be under control. Sheleg kept pace with them, following along a few steps behind, until they reached a large door that he was not permitted to pass. He stayed behind, still carrying the man's shoulder bag. He took a drink from a water fountain in the hall and then sat down in a chair along the wall, waiting to see what would transpire. He was relaxed, but very tired. He closed his eyes, thinking about everything that had happened over the past few days. He opened them again, feeling drowsy and half asleep, and shortly he closed them once more …

IIIIIIIIIII

Sheleg suddenly opened his eyes and saw the tall man standing in front of him with two steaming cups in his hands. He wondered how long he had been sitting there. He had no idea. A few seconds? Minutes? Hours? Apparently he had fallen asleep.

"Would you like some coffee?" the man asked politely.

"Yes, I would, thanks," he nodded.

"My name is Daniel; pleased to meet you," he said, handing Sheleg one of the cups.

"I'm Sheleg, and the pleasure's all mine."

"It's not that often that people help you in this city. I really appreciate it."

"Don't mention it; it was nothing," Sheleg said with a smile as he handed Daniel his bag.

"Do you have a relative or friend in the hospital?" Daniel asked.

"No, I don't. I was just outside and noticed that you could use some help … and how is your wife doing?"

"Very well, thank God. She's resting. Everything happened so fast, but they're fine—my wife and the baby … how incredible. I can't even understand it yet, it all happened so fast!"

"That's great," Sheleg said. "And how about you? How are you doing?"

"It's hard to explain … it's … are you a father?" Daniel asked, trying to find the words.

"No," Sheleg smiled, slowly shaking his head, "but my wife is four months pregnant."

"Oh, that's wonderful. Seeing your child for the first time is … it's an indescribable feeling—like all the love in the world is bubbling up inside of you," Daniel explained. "I know what it's like to be in love, I know how it feels to love my parents, and I know how it feels to love a friend. But this is different. It's so pure. I just felt like crying, and thanking God for showing me that such an immense, perfect emotion existed."

Sheleg looked at him and smiled. He was so sincere that Sheleg could almost feel for himself what Daniel was experiencing. It was a magical moment, and the feeling Daniel had was so overwhelming that he didn't even think twice about talking openly with a perfect stranger he had met only minutes before at the hospital's entrance.

"Everything happened so fast that we didn't even have time to get ready. My wife was scheduled for a cesarean, but then all of a sudden she was having these really strong pains. I called the ambulance, and here we are. She had a normal delivery, in spite of all the predictions. They asked me to step outside for a few minutes as they straightened everything up in there, and while my wife's resting for a bit. If you'd like, we can go back in together and you can meet them both," Daniel offered, smiling.

Sheleg's eyes shone, overwhelmed by the offer. "Thank you, I'm very moved that you would ask me." He hadn't expected this man to be so willing to share such an intimate event.

"You seem like a good man," Daniel observed, just as a nurse stepped out of the room. She told him he could go back in. "Let's go!" he said, clutching his bag.

Sheleg felt nervous. He knew how significant this moment was, and everything had to be just right—he didn't want his presence to break the moment's magic. "What is your son's name?" he asked.

"Michael," Daniel said as Sheleg held the door open.

They went into the room, which was softly lit by a floor lamp in the corner. In the center of the room was a large bed, covered in spotless, white sheets, where Daniel's wife lay with their baby in her arms. Sheleg could not see her face, since she was so absorbed looking at the infant. He decided to wait for a more appropriate moment to introduce himself.

The room was infused with a very peaceful feeling, and even though there were none of the flowers, balloons, or greeting cards usually found in these situations, a palpable, wondrous energy filled the room. Daniel slowly approached the bed and leaned over to gently touch the baby, who remained asleep, his eyes closed.

After a few minutes during which Sheleg was practically invisible, Daniel turned to him and whispered, "Come over here."

He approached the bed with slow steps, almost as if he was floating. As he turned around the end of the bed, he could see the newborn's face, his eyes still closed. The infant portrayed an indescribable innocence, which seemed to come from the peacefulness of knowing that his parents' presence provided a perfect state of protection for him. Still nervous, Sheleg looked closely at the baby as he slowly walked toward the bed. The new mother did not take her eyes off her baby, and for a minute Sheleg felt as if he was trespassing where he didn't belong. He stopped and tried to take a step backward, but he couldn't; he was paralyzed. His feet did not respond, and his body would not do what he wished. He began to tremble all over. His palms were sweating, and his breathing grew more and more labored.

What am I doing here? What do I have to do with this? he wondered.

He felt trapped in the moment. He couldn't understand what was happening. Suddenly he remembered all the circumstances that had brought him to this city—seeing Jose again, receiving the strange message from Jose, his trip to the wilderness, his strange vision of the lynx and the wolf, the attempted assault, running into Gabriel, and the coincidences as the ride back to the city, the ambulance and the taxi that brought him to this hospital. He was still shaking, and the room seemed to grow colder. He felt that something was about to happen, that something was about to be revealed, that what he had been searching so hard for was about to appear. He didn't know what it was, but he would soon find out …

At that moment the woman looked up and gazed at Sheleg. They both froze. It was Allyson, his friend from the purple place. They were both transfixed, stunned. Time stopped, and their lives flashed back before their eyes in just a few seconds, transporting them to the past, when they were both barely two years old. They both relived the same memory …

IIIIIIIIIII

They were at a beach. Papa Kamuela carried Sheleg, while a woman Sheleg now suddenly knew was named Mayea-Harip carried Allyson. There were two other people there, but their faces were blurry. The children both saw those two hug them and say good-bye, walking off toward the ocean and fading away into the horizon …

IIIIIIIIIII

That was all Sheleg and Allyson could remember from that moment. They had been raised separately—Sheleg by Kamuela and Allyson by Mayea-Harip. Neither had ever known who their real parents were, but the love and attention they'd received from their surrogates was so genuine that they hadn't suffered any kind of harm from not having known their biological parents. They had both grown up in cultures very different from what most people experienced, so it was hard for them to explain, among other things, their unusual detachment from their real parents.

Allyson seemed to be coming out of her trance-like state, and she murmured, "Sheleg?"

"Yes," he replied, still in a state of shock. "Yes, it's me. What is this?"

For the first time they understood something they never would have suspected: their imaginary relationship had never been imaginary at all, and the experiences they both had had in that parallel world were as real as that very moment in the hospital. They now knew that they were twins, and they had been brought to this planet by their parents and given to those two beings of a higher state of consciousness named Kamuela and Mayea-Harip.

"Did you see what I saw?" she asked, surprised.

"Yes," Sheleg nodded, still struggling to make sense of what had happened. "I saw Mayea; she had you in her arms. I hadn't remembered her …" He paused for a minute, and then went on, "Well, how could I have remembered something that happened when I was only two, right?" he said, confused, trying to explain something that required no explanation.

"That's what happened to me," Allyson said. "I saw you, and Kamuela, and Mayea … and our parents. I remember now how they disappeared into the horizon."

They were both lost in thought—the riddle of their lives was being solved right in front of them, and it was completely unexpected and totally stunning. Each had always known there were some blank spots in their life histories, but what was being revealed to them now was something far beyond what they ever could have imagined.

"Where could they be now?" Allyson asked, looking at Sheleg.

"I don't know," he answered, "but I wish they were here."

Daniel, disconcerted and not understanding anything that was happening, asked in an increasingly frantic voice, "You two know each other? You're brother and sister? You never told me you had a brother! Who is Kamuela? *What's going on*?"

Allyson gave him a flustered look, since she didn't completely understand what was happening, either. Daniel had always known that his wife was not a typical woman, and he was used to unusual things happening in her life, but this was definitely the strangest thing of all.

Just then a rather large nurse in a white uniform and with a cheerful expression walked in, carrying a box in her hands. Oblivious to what was happening, she said with a friendly smile, "There's a phone call for Mr. Daniel Harlack at the nurse's station. I think it's your mother; it seems she's been trying to reach you on your cell phone but couldn't get through. You probably can't get a signal in the hospital."

"Yes, that's me; thank you," Daniel said. "I'll be right back. Don't go anywhere!" he said to Sheleg and Allyson somewhat incongruously as glanced at his cell phone and then he went to answer the call. "It must have been turned off," he said mostly to himself as he turned it on again and walked out the door.

"This box was just dropped off at reception," the nurse now said, holding out the package to Sheleg. He thanked her and took it. After quickly examining Allyson, the nurse left the room.

"There's a note," Sheleg said, perplexed. He fell quiet.

"What does it say?" Allyson asked, intrigued by Sheleg's continuing silence.

He looked at her and without a word took the note off of the box. After a short pause, he read in a clear voice:

> You are both the most precious thing the universe could have given us. We will see you very soon. With everlasting love,
>
> —Ari-cadu and Sarah

They were both puzzled. It was too much all at once, so they didn't even question how the mysterious package had arrived.

To Sheleg, the name Sarah meant a mother that he had yet to meet, but to Allyson, it had an even greater significance. Years earlier, as Allyson walked through an open-air market, a pleasant-looking elderly woman had come up to her and said, "Don't worry, my daughter; everything will be alright. He's going to be okay. Have faith, and follow everything you believe in."

At the time, her husband Daniel had been undergoing his third month of chemotherapy since a cancerous lesion in his lung had been found. The diagnosis had upended both of their lives, and Allyson had sunk into a state of dark pessimism, dragging her slowly down into a deep depression.

"What do you mean, ma'am?" Allyson asked, confused.

"You know what I mean, because what is pressing down on your heart, enveloping you in sadness, is pressing down on me, too."

Allyson was in a daze. That strange, surreal sensation that had come over her in waves over the past several days—because of her lack of sleep, she'd thought—was now even stronger. She managed to focus her gaze to meet the eyes of the friendly old woman to ask, "But how do you know? How can you know about what I'm going through and how I'm feeling?"

"Are you cold?" the woman asked.

"Yes, a little bit …"

"You see that hill over there?" she said, gesturing toward a verdant hillside that had a mantel of moss and grass draped over its irregular rock formations.

"Yes, I see it."

"Do you have any doubt that it's there?" the old woman asked.

"No," Allyson murmured, eager to hear the old woman repeat her hopeful message.

"Then don't forget what I'm saying to you … everything will pass, everything will be fine. Just be strong, because you two, you and your husband, still have much to do. You'll see that soon, very soon. When your first child is born, you'll have left behind all of the uncertainty and the doubtful moments …"

Those were the only words she had ever heard that very forthright woman called Sarah say. To Allyson, she was like an angel sent down from heaven, giving her the strength to keep going, to meet the very difficult challenge life had put in front of her.

She turned her attention back to the present, in the hospital room. "Open it," Allyson said to Sheleg, anxious to see what the package contained.

He did, and he took out a small, rectangular chest made of wood and a material similar to copper, polished and very shiny. He carefully opened it, and they were both left speechless once again. They couldn't even blink; they were mesmerized. They had only experienced the scent of pine that arose from the chest in one place—on that planet with fine, purple sand and lush trees where they both played happily. They stared at the chest's contents, as Sheleg held it closer to Allyson so they could both touch what was inside.

They felt that fine sand run through their fingers as it slowly dissolved. The feeling once again transported them to that special place where they had been together so many times. They remembered how they would sink into the sand, or how they floated in the craters and the pine trees. The memories flooded into their minds as they silently stared at each other, touching the sand held inside the strange little chest.

A tear rolled down Allyson's cheek. Sheleg wiped at his own moist eyes and kept remembering … they had lived at the very bottom of the craters, which were wide and dark at their tops, but as they went deeper they had a brilliant, infinite light that shone on everything. The place was like the cave Sheleg had visited once with the wise man Ari-cadu, who ended up being his own father. The two siblings now understood that the light came from countless soul-energies fused into one, and even though each had its own particular, wholly unique color, the combination of all of them created an indefinable beauty and perfection in that infinite space. They remembered the day they had been taken to earth and the message their parents had given them before leaving them with Kamuela and Mayea-Harip:

> The essence of life is love; spread that message. The colors you have seen once are infinite. Those you will see now are not. The essence of the universe is one, and you will know you are in the presence of it when the colors you see all around you are infinite once again …

Allyson and Sheleg looked at each other without saying a word; everything was communicated through their minds, through their thoughts. They looked at the baby and clearly understood the message about the essence of life. That small infant was the result of that essence. Allyson and Daniel had given life to the first being procreated by two beings from different worlds—different planets, different universes—moved by that feeling which is the key to unlocking the secrets of infinity.

Now that their true origin had been revealed, Sheleg laughed at the paradox. All that time he had wondered why he had never seen any life beyond the confines of earth on all his travels through the universe, and yet his own reflection in the mirror showed him such alien life. He thought, *And that's how it so often is, since we are constantly searching for answers in the most remote places, not realizing that the answers can be found within ourselves—within our bodies, in our minds, and in our souls …*

"Daniel told me that his name is Michael," Sheleg said as he gently touched the baby.

The child's mother said, "Yes, Michael is the name we decided on."

"Why that name?"

"When I found out I was pregnant, I asked God to always keep the baby healthy and peaceful. We were afraid, because Daniel had had some health problems in the past. That very night while I was asleep, I dreamed that three angels came up to me and told me not to worry, that they would always watch over him. The three angels were named Mia, Charley, and Ely, so we took the first letters of each name and came up with 'Mi-Cha-El.' Michael."

Sheleg dropped to his knees, his head pressed to his sister's arm as tears ran down his cheek. He felt a sudden wave of peacefulness course through him. He knew now that his three friends were once again a part of his life, confirming in the most unexpected way that they were alright. After so many years, he could finally close that sad chapter of his life that had begun all those years ago with that horrible explosion.

Before Allyson could ask Sheleg what was the matter, they heard hurried footsteps approaching in the hallway. The door swung open, and Sheleg heard a familiar voice. It was his friend, Jose. He was breathing hard, and Daniel was right behind him.

He asked Allyson to forgive him for the intrusion, and went on, "I lied to you, Sheleg. I know it's crazy, but I lied to you. I'm so sorry ..."

Sheleg was surprised by his friend's sudden presence. He listened, astonished, as Jose explained, "That day we talked in the park, I really did wake up feeling really bad. I didn't know what was wrong with me. Like I told you, I was very depressed. So after I took a long shower, I talked to Mary about a story I had read the night before about a Tibetan goddess. I don't know why, but somehow the conversation got around to your arrival in New York, and I told Mary I had some doubts that anything was going to happen because of your visit. She told me that I was probably right, that maybe nothing would happen. But she said that in any case she was happy, because she had seen over the past few days many positive changes in me, and that was more than enough for her.

"I insisted that your arrival here would have been much more interesting if something really dramatic happened aside from just a spiritual transformation in my life. So I decided to put what you had tried to teach me to the test. Since I was feeling really down that morning, I thought it was a chance to see how you would face the situation," Jose said as everyone listened intently to his story.

"That's why I asked to meet you in the park. But I made up that story; I wanted to see what you would do, if you would be overwhelmed with doubts and confusion too. But a little while ago, something really weird happened to me. I thought hard about what I had told you that day, and then I started to get really scared. At first, I knew you weren't going to do anything bad. But then I felt really upset, and I wondered what would happen if you did anything extreme. A chill ran up my spine, and I understood just how crazy what I had done was. I sat down in the living room and asked for a chance to make amends. My conscience was telling me that I should never manipulate anyone, much less for the purpose of creating chaos and confusion."

Just then Daniel's cell phone rang, and he answered. Jose went over to Sheleg and said quietly, "Please forgive me; I'm so ashamed, but that morning I lost my way. I let myself be guided by confusion, and I couldn't control myself. I wanted to see what would happen if I put you in the same kind of situation that I was in—one of doubt, and fear. I wanted to see just how valuable your life principles were when unexpected circumstances came up," Jose concluded.

"That happens pretty often," Sheleg answered, "and the best thing you can do at those times is smile in the face of those feelings. Then they will gradually go away on their own, since you're not nurturing them with fear and confusion. You understand that what you did was wrong; no one has the right to put anyone else to the test, much less in the way that you did."

"Yes, I understand. And believe me, I've learned my lesson …" Jose acknowledged, trailing off.

"By the way," Sheleg asked, "how did you know I was here?"

"This is the hospital that was on the piece of paper I gave you in the park. That day, I called up a friend of mine who's a doctor and asked him about the births they had scheduled for this date. I told him I was doing some research, gathering statistical data for the company, to avoid unnecessary questions. He sent me a list by fax, and I selected this birth." Jose handed a piece of paper to Sheleg, and he read what was written on it out loud.

Allyson, quietly piecing the story together from her bed, looked at Sheleg, who was surprised by how things had developed. She confirmed for Sheleg what the note said. "That's right, I had a cesarean scheduled for 10:30 tonight. I had asked the doctor to schedule it for that time for astrological reasons … well … you know …" she said, gazing at Daniel, who was by now used to his wife making plans in that way. "But this afternoon I started having some really sharp pains, so we called an ambulance. Once we got here, the doctors decided I could have a normal birth, so that's what we did," she finished, cuddling her baby, who was sleeping deeply, removed for everything happening around him.

"I see that you got here with several hours to spare," Sheleg said to Jose, glancing at a clock on the wall. It was almost 8:00.

"Of course, since you yourself told Gabriel to call me!" Jose said, a bit confused.

"What do you mean? Gabriel?" Sheleg said, even more confused. "I didn't say anything to Gabriel about calling you!"

Jose hadn't paid attention to Sheleg's comment, and he continued, "Yes, the guy who works in my office. He told me he ran into you in the street, and you asked him to call me. Like I told you, I was in my living room begging for forgiveness for what I had done, and then the phone rang. It was Gabriel, telling me you were on your way over here to do what I had asked you to do. So I dropped everything and came over here as fast as I could to explain to all of you the situation. Ah! And by the way, he also told me that you were going to give me something you brought back from the mountain …"

Still completely stunned, Sheleg slowly shook his head as he reached into his bag and took out the stick that the lynx had given to him in the mountains. He handed it to Jose.

"What's this?" the man exclaimed.

"This is something that will always remind you of the consequences lies and manipulation can have," Sheleg said simply, still thinking of Gabriel. *Who was that strange person? An angel? The archangel, Gabriel? Who knows …?* Sheleg looked at the sky out the window and thanked him for his help, and his presence …

The room was silent, since nothing that was happening was easy to make sense of. But that creative force that is always present in everything showed everyone gathered in the hospital room that everything that seems real could possibly be an illusion, and everything that seems like an illusion could be what's real.

Sheleg said in a clear voice, "God works in mysterious ways, and that's how He brought us all together here. Each one with his own history, which we have to learn from so that together, one day, we can all see those infinite colors that will let us redraw again any gray story in any human life."

IIIIIIIIIII

In the dark night sky seen through the room's window, three bright shooting stars blazed across the firmament, disappearing into the infinite.

CHAPTER 9

One last detail

"Nothing is irreversible."

Only through raising our consciousness
can we benefit from the law of cause and effect,
changing the course of our own destiny.

~ ~ ~

Allow me to introduce myself. I am Kamuela, and like Sheleg's, my life has also included many intense, meaningful moments. It may be hard to understand that my soul is not restricted to a single body, but that's how it is. Since my spirit knows no freedom because it also knows no restriction, it does not recognize good just as it does not recognize evil. Nor does it differentiate between what is generally considered ugly and what is called pretty, because where I am, none of that exists. As you will discover, that which you call a body does not exist here, either. That is what this place is like, where one day you and I will meet. When? I don't know; that only depends on you … but I'll be waiting, because I am the eternity.

The moment has come for me to say good-bye. But before I do, I would like to tell you what happened to me after I got into the taxi that took Sheleg to the hospital the day that Michael was born …

Three hours earlier …

"Excuse me, are you available?" I asked the taxi driver who was parked outside the hospital.

"That guy that just got out still has to pay me; I'm waiting for him to come back," he said, gesturing toward Sheleg, who was slowly walking toward the ambulance that had brought Daniel and Allyson to the hospital.

"Don't worry about it. I'll pay for him."

"But it's almost twenty dollars!" the driver said, surprised.

"It's no problem. Let's go; he probably doesn't even remember you're out here," I said with a grin.

"Okay!" We both got into the taxi and I handed the driver the money. "Thanks a lot," he said as we drove away from the hospital.

I could see the cab reflected in the rounded, glass-walled building on my left as we disappeared from the hospital's view.

"Where do you want to go?" the driver, who as you know went by the name Tony, asked politely.

I replied, "I have to be back at the hospital later, but right now I have some time to kill."

"Alright. Would you like me to just drive around the city?"

"Yes, that sounds great."

Keeping the conversation going, Tony asked, "Do you have a family member in the hospital?"

"Yes, my daughter; she's about to have a baby any minute now."

Tony was surprised with the answer. "I know this is none of my business, sir, but wouldn't you rather be with her right now?"

"Yes, I'd love to, but it's not the right moment."

"What do you mean, if you don't mind my asking?"

"I promised my wife that we would share this moment together, and I don't want to be there if she can't be there."

"Oh, I understand … Do you want me to go pick up your wife? I wouldn't mind at all!" the driver offered generously.

I smiled. "I would like to, but the problem is I don't know where she is."

"So if you don't know where she is, how are you going to get back to her, if she's not around?" Tony asked, very puzzled. "I mean … I'm sorry, but now I really don't understand what you're talking about."

"It's a very long story, my friend, but thank you for asking," I replied with a smile, since at that moment only I could understand these apparent incongruities. We were silent for several minutes. The driver clearly didn't understand what was going on at all, and soon he began asking me questions to try and figure it out.

"Where are you from?"

"I come from some islands very far from here, in the Pacific Ocean."

"Hmmm, that is very far, indeed! I've always wanted to visit that part of the world. The Philippines, Fiji, Thailand … I've seen pictures and heard stories from customers who I pick up who have been there."

"Yes, it's a world away, with different customs and a whole other lifestyle. But it's interesting to see those contrasts up close, and see how similar we humans are, and how different at the same time."

"Very interesting …" Tony said. He appeared to think for a moment. "You know, you really remind me of a woman who works in our home, helping out my wife with our granddaughter. My daughter and her husband both work during the day, so we help take care of their little girl."

"Oh? Why do I remind you of this woman?"

"You have similar features and, with all respect, you also talk the same way. You're both rather unusual … pleasant people, but very unusual!" he said with a chuckle as he looked at me through the rearview mirror. "I think she's from Hawaii or somewhere near there," he said, unsure.

"*Ha*!" I shouted happily. "Well alright, Tony, my friend. I think you could be the answer to what I've been searching for," I said, putting a hand on his shoulder.

"What are you talking about?" He asked, surprised.

"I mean that woman you just told me about is my wife, Mayea-Harip!" I replied.

Tony slammed on the brakes and pulled over to the curb. "How do you know Mayea? Is this some kind of joke?" he asked, completely bewildered.

"This is no joke," I said, smiling, "and I'd love to explain everything."

"Well, I'd love to hear it, because this is the strangest thing that's ever happened to me in my whole life!"

Without any preamble and knowing how he would react, I said simply, "My name is Kamuela, and I serve as an intermediary between the inhabitants of other planets and this one. After a long retreat, Mayea and I agreed that we would meet again when our first grandchild was born."

"Mister, are you trying to drive me crazy? What are you talking about? What other planets?" he asked with an anguished expression, waving his hands.

Trying to hold in my laughter and mustering up the most serious expression in my repertoire, I answered, "We're going to go find Mayea, and on the way I'll tell you the whole story, okay?"

"Well, yes, of course … I'd like to hear the whole story. But please, just down-to-earth facts! No flying saucers! No extraterrestrials nonsense! And no baloney! Okay?"

"Okay," I agreed, and then I began, "She and I took charge of two children and raised them as our own ever since they were little. Mayea raised Allyson, and I raised Sheleg, since their parents come from a very far, far away place called—"

Tony sighed loudly and interrupted, "Please don't start with that again! For God's sake, don't start with me again!"

"Alright, alright, alright," I said, patting his shoulder. "If you want, I won't say anything else until we get to the house. We'll pick up Mayea and go back to the hospital. Then we can calmly explain everything, okay?

"Perfect," answered Tony, twisting his head around to look at me in the eyes.

I couldn't contain myself. "But let me tell you … I think your wife, Rebecca, has too many things to explain to you, too …"

The End (… is just the beginning)

A final thought

The journeys that we learn from, the places where we study, or the mountains where we take refuge are nothing more than metaphors, because in life, each person follows their own path and goes to visit their own mountains. Each one of us is a wholly unique, inimitable piece in an enormous, universal puzzle, where we must find our own place and our own reason for being.

That universal puzzle needs us, just like we need it. The only way to complete it is to join the pieces together; all the pieces must unite. That's where responsibility, respect and consideration become a fundamental part of our lives, since even though each person has their own path and their own destiny, that path can't be traveled with no connection to others …

Made in United States
Orlando, FL
12 November 2024

53762494R00080